A MORBID OBSESSION

A Grim Reaper Comedy Adventure

Riya Aarini

A Morbid Obsession: A Grim Reaper Comedy Adventure

ISBN: 978-1-956496-48-2 (eBook)

ISBN: 978-1-956496-47-5 (Paperback)

www.riyapresents.com

Take it from the Grim Reaper:

Never run out of vodka.

I swung open the door, the second time that day, to another bouquet of red roses, with buds on the verge of blooming and surrounded by clusters of baby's breath. The little white flowers symbolized thoughtfulness, so the mysterious sender who sent me these bouquets was sincere in their affections. So sincere, as I'd just received six bouquets yesterday and four the day before that.

None of the cards that came with the bouquets was signed. All I noticed was one red heart in the bottom right corners—and nothing else, no signature, no printed name, nada, zilch.

Who could my admirer be?

Since my recent rise to fame, it could've been anyone.

Valentine's Day was in a few days, so flowers expressing love and devotion were unsurprising this time of year. I hummed a merry tune as I sought a proper receptacle for them.

I dropped the bouquet of roses in an empty vodka bottle, filled it half with water, and stood back to admire the sight of romance and inhale the fragrance of love. After the second bouquet I'd received, I'd run out of vases and had to improvise. After all, I wasn't used to getting flowers from anyone.

Another bouquet sat in a teapot on the kitchen counter, which dampened my spirits slightly; I longed to make a cup of hot tea this wintry afternoon and owned only one teapot. But on a good note, the red flowers brightened my kitchen so I tolerated the mild annoyance. Two bouquets also sat in a pitcher, five in mason jars, and two in my rainboots. Red roses filled every nook and cranny of my rental home.

Someone must've really admired me. A *secret* admirer. How romantic, with an air of intrigue. Nothing felt more enticing. Or it could've been several secret admirers, with various love bugs responsible for sending me all these roses over the past three days with a red heart scribbled in the corner. A light tingling zipped through my bones.

Then my phone chirped. I checked my text messages. It was Death, asking me to see him in the office tomorrow morning.

I wrung my hand bones, suddenly drenched in sweat. What did I do now? Surely the boss wasn't about to rebuke me. I'd been doing my job perfectly and even enhanced it a bit by sending my clients pre-pickup text messages ever since I got my first phone. I'd built a rapport with the souls

I collected, making their journey to the other side pleasant. Death couldn't have been angry about that.

Or maybe he'd gotten mad about me casually writing off my multiple device purchases on my expense report. Any little thing could've set him off.

Trying to distract myself from all the possibilities that the boss could call me out on, I prepared dinner. After chowing down a hearty bowl of creamy pasta Alfredo and watching black-and-white reruns of *The Three Stooges* on the television, I checked my phone and turned in for the night.

But I didn't sleep. Though I should have. My bed was strewn with red rose petals. I literally walked on velvety-soft rose petals, tender and luxurious under my ancient feet bones, that had fallen all over the carpets. The night exuded floral scents that wafted through the entire house, lifting my spirits. The night was magical—all ruined by my boss asking me to see him and failing to explain why.

The sun rose by morning, but I couldn't. Bone tired, I resisted dragging myself out of bed to face whatever Death had in store for me.

I fought my desire to sleep in and avoid the boss. At eight o'clock I yanked off the covers, threw my leg bones over the side of the bed, and grunted. Stumbling out of bed, I sauntered into the kitchen.

As I prepared my morning espresso in my brushed, stainless steel espresso machine—a lovely workplace gift from Life for my 708th birthday—the doorbell rang.

"Come on. This early?" I grumbled.

I opened the door, only to be greeted with yet another bouquet of red roses. Upon mumbling a quick thank you to the flower delivery guy, I brought the flowers inside and scratched my skull. Where was I about to put this?

I found an old chemistry set lying around, so I cut down the stems and inserted them into the various glass beakers. Black roses would've complemented the unique makeshift vases better than these red blooms. But who's lookin'? The flowers in the beakers gave off a cool, experimental vibe.

I dashed off to the office, muttering to myself like a lunatic during the whole commute. It was what I did when worry consumed me.

Upon reaching the office, I knocked on Death's door.

"Yeah?" came his resounding voice. "Come in."

Inching the door open—I didn't want my face bones blown off by his fury—I poked my skull inside.

"You wanted to see me, boss?" My voice came out puny and weak.

Death waved his mighty hand, welcoming me in. "Reaper, yes. Have a seat." He motioned for me to sit down in one of the chairs across from his rustic, bristlecone pine desk, which must've been thousands of years old. The boss had been around a long time, and his office furniture showed it.

Staring at him from across the desk, I quivered. I loved my job, the amazing places it took me, and all the personalities attached to the souls I got to meet. It was fulfilling on so many levels. I'd held it for seven hundred years and wasn't keen on losing a job I fancied so much. Since I recently integrated texting into the collection of souls, my job was all the more fun. Death couldn't do this to me. He couldn't take away everything that brought me nonstop joy and satisfaction.

"Listen, Reaper," he started to say, his gaze dropping to his desk.

Oh no. His voice sounded calm and collected. I knew it was coming. He couldn't even look at me. I'd lose it all right here in this seat.

"I've known you for a long time."

I braced myself. Firings always started this way, a harkening back to when it all started.

"I've come to trust you not only as a valuable employee but as a member of my social sphere."

What?

He leaned forward and looked me in the eye. Being to being. "I've got a favor to ask."

A favor?

I shook my face bones to clear my skull. "Uh, sure, boss. What is it?"

"See, I've got a hurricane scheduled for Valentine's Day, February 14, along the northern coast of Sumatra." He looked away, leaned back in his swivel chair, and brought his fingers into a steeple position in front of his massive chest.

"It's going to keep me pretty busy. It'll be big, very big, of epic proportions. It'll go down in the history books. But I don't want to leave my gal lonely. Not on Valentine's Day."

He turned to look at me. "I'd like you to take Life out, maybe a little dancing. You know, show her a good time. How 'bout it?" Death gave me a smile. "If you're free, that is."

That was it?

I stumbled over my words. "Uh, yeah, sure, boss. I'm free. I'd be happy to take Life out."

Death leaned back and clapped his hands. "That's great. Really great. I knew I could count on you, Reaper."

"Is that all, boss?"

"Yep, that's it! Thanks again, Reaper."

I calmly got up from my seat, then slowly closed the office door behind me. As I leaned my spine against it, the empty insides of my rib cage began to heave, as if ready to explode in a spectacular firework show. But this time it was because Death asked me to take Life out on a date. The cosmic force of my dreams. The most gorgeous being in the universe, who made every bone in my skeleton gush with effervescent happiness with merely a look. The light of my dark existence. The shimmer of hope in utter bleakness.

Life was my secret, eternal crush.

And I was about to take her out in five days.

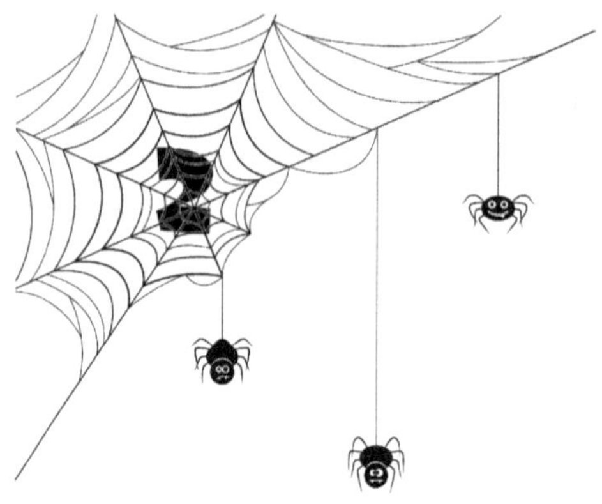

Sunday evening couldn't have arrived soon enough. I steamed and pressed my black cloak until not a wrinkle was left, then sewed the rips and tears that had widened into gaping holes over the centuries. I polished and whitened my teeth, so I could give Life a gleaming, picture-perfect smile. I'd been smiling all day preparing for tonight—a big night, the biggest night of my existence. I'd get to dance with the most beautiful cosmic force that pervaded the entire universe.

I gave myself one last look in the mirror. Smoothing out the ends of my cloak with my sweaty hand bones, I sauntered out of my rental to pick up Life. I arrived at her stately home and rang the doorbell. She opened the door immediately, giving me a smile that lit up the evening like a moonbeam.

She stood in a shimmery green off-the-shoulder gown, the color of lush moss, with dainty spaghetti straps over her glistening shoulders. Her untamed, fiery red hair curled like wisps of wild bonfire smoke. Gazing at her figure, curvaceous as a perfectly crafted hourglass, and her round, luminescent face was like kayaking through the breathtaking green waters of Las Vegas's Emerald Cave. Every inch of her was a mesmerizing sight to behold. I stood unavoidably hypnotized.

"Ready?" she asked, her emerald green eyes lighting up.

I rejoiced, observing this blissful vision before me, and resisted interrupting my moment of rapture. But the night was young, and I kept the lady waiting. Returning her smile, I replied, "Let's go!"

We had reservations at the posh steakhouse. The waiter, dressed to match the atmospheric elegance of rich blacks and browns of the walls and exotic decor from locales near and far, seated us right away. Our table gave us a panoramic view of the moonlit lake.

"Look, the moonlight is reflecting on the water," I pointed out to Life.

She leaned over to look out of the window. "A splendid sight."

Her inching nearer to me over the table, even for those few seconds, drove me slightly mad.

She placed her order and unfolded the white napkin over her lap.

Clearly, she knew the proper etiquette for a five-star restaurant, so I followed her lead and did the same. Posh restaurants weren't my cup of tea. I preferred happy hour at the local roadhouse, with cheap steak, fries, and a beer, where I always brought home leftovers.

She called the sommelier to the table and asked for the house's best red wine. The sommelier recommended a cabernet sauvignon.

"It's nice and dry. Rich and deep, one sip will linger in your mouth," she advised.

"Let's have a bottle," Life said, smiling at me, then looking back up at the wine expert.

"Certainly," the sommelier replied and left.

Life and I enjoyed light conversation about the unique ambiance of the restaurant. Then we discussed how hardworking Death was and the hurricane that kept him away that evening. Once our filet mignons arrived, we continued conversing over dinner about Death's perfectionism, his stalwart commitment to his task over the past four billion years, and the importance of his role in the wide universe.

"Nothing could exist without him," Life said in between forkfuls of juicy steak she lightly dipped in her little tub of peppercorn sauce. "I don't even have a chance."

"Death sure is a central figure in the scheme of things," I said, taking a sip of my cabernet. It really did coat the mouth and linger.

I didn't know much about wines. I was more of a straight vodka guy. One shot delivered a mean kick. But Life embodied classiness and deserved the extraordinary cuisine and exceptional service this swanky five-star restaurant had to offer. I was glad to make it happen this Valentine's Day.

Upon finishing our dinner and wine, I took her to the Next World Ballroom across town.

I offered my elbow bone to Life, and we walked in together. It was like entering a heavenly realm, not only because of the stunning being on my arm bone, but because the ballroom was bathed in pure white: glossy white ceilings, multitiered crystal chandeliers hanging like icicles in the middle of a frosty winter, and a shiny tile dance floor that beckoned everyone—even a reaper with two left feet bones.

"What a fantastic ballroom!" Life exclaimed with a clap of her hands.

"It sure is nice. What'd you say we hit the dance floor?"

Life grabbed me by the hand bone and rushed me to the middle of the floor. As the Cuban music sounded, she danced the cha-cha. She pressed her elbow against my elbow bone and stepped to the side, rocked, cha-cha'd, and did it all over again. Feeling the rhythmic Latin music pulse through my bones, I twirled her. She wriggled her lithe body like a snake. She spun around and around, making me dizzy, as my finger bones grasped her warm hand above her head. I twisted my skeleton chaotically, flailed my arm bones, and grinned, trying to look like I knew what I was doing.

After a few minutes of unparalleled bliss, the music abruptly changed. The bandonion produced a fast tango melody that Life couldn't resist. She flung one arm around my cervical spine and gazed directly into my empty eye sockets. I shivered. She threw her arms to the side, dropped her body down, then thrust her leg between my leg bones. In a flash, she hoisted herself up and spun around and around.

I flipped her up in the air. She laughed. I didn't know how I managed to do it or my other moves. I'd never danced the tango before, or any style of ballroom dance, in my entire existence. But the tango music had its way with me. She shot her leg straight up, then tangled her leg in my leg bones. Her long locks whipped across my face bones; I inhaled their delicious floral scent. She did the horizontal splits in midair as the violin played and I held her arms. The ecstasy blew my skull.

The reverie lasted until the music changed, this time to a slow fox-trot. Life threw her head back, as I held her powdery soft arms. Carrying her head in such an awkward position during the dance must've felt awfully uncomfortable. I wanted to ask, "Are you okay like that?" But, caught up in the rapture of being in the arms of this amazing life-force, I didn't. She performed a pivot turn, then a quarter turn to the left. We promenaded to the steady, boring music. The movements were slow, slow, slow, then quick, quick, quick. But it failed to be as riveting as the tango.

Again the music switched, this time to a waltz. As Life rolled onto her toes and stepped to the side, my cloak started to drag across the floor. She accidentally stepped on it as we closed. I heard the cloth rip and grimaced. Thankfully, she was too absorbed in the music to hear. It'd have turned me red in the face bones had she noticed. I kept waltzing until the fabulous night ended.

Tired out, we walked together, arm in arm bone, off the dance floor. Life was all giggles, which was contagious. Despite not wanting my sensational night to end, I dutifully took her home. She thanked me for a lovely time, and, slightly dazed at the awesomeness I'd just experienced, I returned to my rental.

Upon entering my porch, I tripped over more bouquets of roses. Eh, I left them there.

What a night. For someone with two left feet bones, I wasn't half bad on the dance floor. How I wished more than anything that I could do it again, not with just anyone, but with Life.

I dropped my tired bones into bed and began to dream. What were the odds? Life and me? Nah, she was off-limits. Death and Life were inseparable, yin and yang, light and dark. One could not exist without the other. Wherever Life was, Death wasn't too far behind. They completed—complemented—each other. But me, carrying out Death's orders, made me a close second. If Death ever lost interest, I'd surrender to Life in an eternal second.

Still imagining the possibilities, I sighed and drifted off to sleep.

Upon completing my massive rounds of soul pickups that Monday morning, attributable to Death's latest hurricane, I returned to the office. Ever since the boss started sending me my schedule as a text message attachment, I didn't see the need to hold on to the voluminous piles of paper schedules.

I opened the two metal doors to the eternal file cabinet and glanced up at the hundred-foot-high stacks of papers crammed inside. The paper schedules from the past seven hundred years, piled one on top of the other, threatened to tumble out at any opportune moment and create chaotic disorganization.

"I'll fix that," I muttered to myself and thought to scan the paper files into digital records that would endure forever. If any soul griped about it not being their time, the digital records served as proof of their destiny.

Paper schedules could've disintegrated in inhospitable conditions, leaving me in a helpless position. Death's lists of souls to pick up were as valuable as receipts for major purchases and should've been stored with utmost care. I never knew when a situation demanded I refer back to them.

Climbing a ladder, I gathered the schedules lying at the top, climbed back down, then proceeded to scan them at the scanner at the other end of the office. As I scanned, I smacked my mouth. It felt dry.

"I need some water." I paused my task and strolled over to the water cooler. As a steady stream of cold water trickled into my paper cup, Death walked by.

"Hey, Reaper!" He came over. "Thanks for taking my gal out last night."

"Oh, sure, no problem, boss."

"She had a great time." Death leaned his muscular arm casually against the wall. "She said you were quite the gentleman."

Still filling my cup, I lowered my eye sockets. "Well, I try."

Death stood upright again, his massive chest puffing out. "Listen, I've got a big monsoon coming up in Bangladesh in October." His eyes widened, electricity almost seemed to shoot out of him, and he made wide sweeping gestures with his arms. "It's going to be epic. *E-P-I-C*. I mean, nobody will forget it."

Blasé, I looked to the side.

"I'll be pretty busy again. You know how time-consuming it is to orchestrate a grand-scale natural disaster like that. Life will be left all lonesome at home." His dark eyes grew misty and he looked off into the distance. He was really enamored.

He turned to me again but switched to an upbeat tone. "So, I was hoping you could take Life out again on Sweetest Day, the day of my epic monsoon. Show her a good time, you know, keep her spirits up."

My eye sockets shot up to meet his smiling face. "Uh, really? I mean, yes, I'd be happy to!"

"Good." Death rubbed his hands together. "I'll let her know to expect you then." He grabbed my shoulder bone and rubbed it with his mighty hand. It sorta hurt.

"Thanks, Reaper. I always knew I could count on you. Remember to bring this up during your next performance review." Still smiling, he winked, and walked away.

My empty insides fluttered light and free. Little ol' me was going to take Life out again.

Instantly, I became aware of a cold sensation.

The water still poured from the cooler, overflowing from the cup and onto the carpet.

"Drats!"

I released the lever and pulled my arm bones back. The bottom hem of my cloak was soaked with water.

"I can't work like this."

I decided to go home and change into something dry.

I returned home to a foul odor permeating every inch of my rental. The overpowering smell had whacked me in the face bones as soon as I'd walked in.

"The roses." It's as if all the roses had dropped dead in the past two hours.

The red blooms had turned an ugly black and drooped pathetically, their stems covered with a layer of greenish slime. Instead of a pleasant fragrance, the dead roses emitted a nasty stench that made my empty insides turn. Granted, I'd been around death long enough, but I never tolerated it in my personal residence.

A thorough cleaning was in store.

Before I got down to scrubbing my place, I headed to the bathroom and took off my damp cloak. A hair dryer sat in the cabinet below. I didn't know why it was there, considering not a strand of hair grew out of my skull. Maybe it came with the rental. Regardless, I blew hot air over the wet sections of my cloak. Then I hung it up on a line in the backyard to fully air-dry. It was a chilly February day, but the bright sunshine would still give my cloak a nice fresh scent.

In nothing but my bare skeleton, I got down to cleaning, all the while daydreaming of my upcoming date with Life in a few months' time. The anticipation of her company during dinner and dancing lifted my spirits to a height so high that I couldn't bring it down. I didn't need to anyway. I rather fancied existing in my imagination—a vivid imagination that would become a delicious reality come Sweetest Day.

Humming a light tune of decadent love and romance, I emptied the teapot, watering can, rain boots, and vodka bottles stuffed with dead, wilting, stinking roses.

One of the vodka bottles stopped me in my tracks. It was a Polish-made vodka with a 192 proof that hit me right in the abdominal cavity when I drank it. I had several empty vodka bottles lined up on my windowsill. Who needed an interior designer when I could do just as good of a job myself? Holding the clear bottle in the air, it reminded me that I could use a sip. But I'd run out. Salivating for the strong stuff, I set the bottle down and distracted myself with more cleaning, humming, and daydreaming. Besides the vodka, stunning Life was on my mind that early afternoon.

Upon gathering the hordes of decayed, smelly rose bouquets, I threw the mess into an extra large, black plastic garbage bag and set it against the door. On my knee bones, I scrubbed the floors until they were sudsy, then rinsed them until they sparkled. I stood up and wiped down the walls. Every surface that a bouquet or even a petal had touched received a thorough washing with a powerful disinfectant cleaner.

Standing back with a sponge in my hand bones and a damp towel hanging over my shoulder bone, I admired my work. The place looked and smelled fantastically clean. I smiled to myself.

As I praised my immaculate rental, I heard a shuffle.

"What was that?" I whipped my skull around.

It sounded again, like it came from the thick bushes out front.

"I can't check it out like this. I need my cloak." I rushed to the backyard and grabbed it. I put it on as I approached the front bay window. A shadowy figure meandered across the bushes.

I scratched my skull. Whatever it was, it was too big and lumbering to be a squirrel or a chipmunk or even a cat.

The sounds just as quickly quieted, and the shadowy movements disappeared.

"Eh, must've been a large stray dog chasing something in the bushes." The little suburb on the Atlantic coast where my current rental was located held a reputation for being quiet and safe. I had no reason to fear wrongdoers in these parts.

I dismissed the strange sounds and sights. My final chore for the day was to take out the trash bag filled with decayed roses. I swung open the front door, grabbed the bag, and was about make my way to the metal trash can on the side of the house when the cause of all the commotion minutes earlier appeared.

She stood just beyond the porch, on the sidewalk, facing me in her head-to-toe skintight black fake-leather leggings and a fitting wraparound sweater-shirt, her cleavage bursting out like a cow's udders. Long black boots crawled up to the edges of her pudgy knees. She wore charcoal black lipstick, overdone black eyeliner, multiple facial piercings, and a nauseating, sunny smile that refused to leave.

A lump formed in my hyoid bone. The trash bag in my hand bones dropped to the ground. I began to hyperventilate. My skull grew dizzy. Disbelieving what I saw, I peered closer at the dark sight before me.

I stood dazed, until my words simply erupted.

"E-Elvira?

"Wh-what're you doing here?" Creepy bells, resembling Hitchcock music, started sounding in my skull.

"I traveled all the way from Italy for you."

Oh? All the way from that tiny, abandoned Mediterranean village?

"How-how'd you find me?" I asked, shrinking in my doorway.

"Nothing escapes love."

Eh? Did she say *love*? My hand bones impulsively grabbed the doorframe to steady myself.

"Do you like my roses?"

"*You* sent me all those roses?" I looked down at the trash bag, crumpled pathetically at my side. She'd scribbled those little hearts on every one of the notes, all of which I'd tossed along with the dead, stinky roses.

"Of course, *amore mio*. Who else?"

She eyed me with a sort of menacing glare. My skeleton trembled like it was January in the Arctic.

"You *do* have no one else, no?"

I mumbled something, neither yes nor no, just bumbled like a lunatic.

"Oh, *amore mio*, I didn't mean to upset you. Come, I would like to show you something."

She reached out her fleshy hand toward me, as if expecting me to take it and hop over some grassy fields of flowers with her to an amazing earthly haven she intended to take me.

I stood immobilized and didn't accept it. I refused.

"Oh, you're shy."

She pouted her black lips and made a sad face.

"Come, I promise you something you will surely love." She smiled and tilted her head.

I looked at her expressionless and didn't budge.

"Oh, don't be afraid. It is something you'll like." She paused to assess my response or lack of one. "I have vodka . . . on my boat." She kept grinning her black lipstick grin.

I lifted myself on my toe bones. "You have vodka? And a boat?" Vodka was my savior, and a boat was integral to my profession for the past seven hundred years. And she had both? I leaned toward her but stopped myself. No, no. I wasn't going anywhere with Elvira, even if she had the good stuff.

"Come on, it is proof 192." She blinked her heavily lined dark eyes.

"How did you know I like vodka?" I asked her.

Elvira twisted her stout body and glanced at my windowsill. "Women know things about their men."

Their men? I didn't buy it.

Then she reached her arm into the bushes.

Not knowing what havoc she was about to introduce, I instinctively followed her chubby arm with my gaze. She pulled out a tall clear bottle with a skinny red neck.

"There's more where this came from," she said waving the full bottle of vodka in front of me. I couldn't take my eye sockets off it.

I salivated. In her grip was the strongest spirit available in the States. I reached one arm bone out toward it. She pulled the bottle away, then curled her index finger and summoned me toward her. I couldn't resist just one drink. She twisted off the bottle cap and, again from the bushes, brought out a small shot glass. She poured me a stiff drink. I accepted it and swigged down the liquor.

"Ah, that was good," I said, and closed my eyes and smacked my mouth.

"Come with me, *amore mio*," she beckoned.

No longer resisting, I followed her, almost as if I was in a trance. All the while, my arm bones reached out to the bottle in her hand for another shot.

Elvira had taken me a few blocks away to the dock on the oceanside port. Still holding the precious bottle, she said, "All the vodka you want is in there." She pointed to a boat.

My eye sockets widened. On the side of the boat was written in big red letters *Amore Reaper*.

"You named your boat after me?" I asked as my jaw dropped.

Smiling, she twisted her body back and forth coyly and replied, "To show you my love. Let us enter." She helped me onto the boat with one hand, and my gaze stayed on the bottle of vodka in her other hand.

"I know a lot about boats," I told her as I looked around hers.

She took me to the bow. "The ocean is so calm."

Only at this very moment.

Then she led me down the stairs to the cabin belowdecks.

I was impressed by the luxury.

The two sofas on either side of the cabin were a soft cream white with nautical-colored pillows arranged across their cushions. The chestnut brown wood gleamed, as if it had just been shined. Three small lights shone from the ceiling of the cabin. The angled windows offered wide views of the Atlantic.

She sat down on one of the sofas and patted the cushion next to hers. "Come, *amore mio*. Have a seat near me." She waved the vodka bottle in front of her.

Eyeing it, I rushed over to be near the liquor.

"Let me make good on my promise."

"Huh?"

"As I said, I promised you more vodka. I'll get it now." She pulled open the door to the compact refrigerator next to the sofa and brought out a bottle of the strongest spirits around. From the drawer, she grabbed a glass. She poured me a stiff drink. I guzzled the sublime concoction like there was no tomorrow. I closed my eyes, immersing myself in the intoxicating effects.

Oddly, I felt a bit woozy. This had never happened to me before, even when I downed the hardest liquors. The cabin started to spin. Elvira's grinning face grew blurrier and blurrier in front of my wobbly skeleton. She'd given me an extra strong drink with a briny, funky flavor—something I'd never tasted in vodka before. Everything went slowly gray, then pitch-dark.

In seconds, I passed out on the sofa.

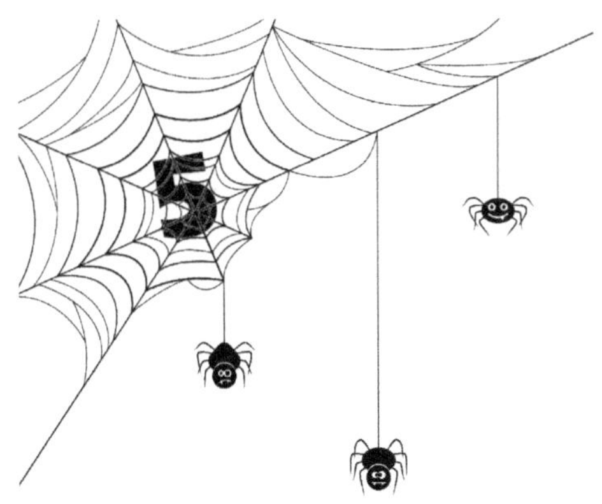

The morning sunlight, reflecting off the surface of the water, flickered through the windows. I rose up from the boat sofa, where I'd been lying all night. Still a bit groggy, I tried to give my stiff arm bones a stretch. But they felt strangely tight and didn't budge.

I glanced down, startled to find a thick rope wrapped eight times around my arm bones and skeleton and four times around both my ankle bones. "What in the afterworld is going on?"

Then I heard an intolerable, high-pitched noise, like a limpkin making its piercing, grating, screeching sound to mark its territory near the marshes. "I sing of love, Reaper . . .lalala. . .*ti amo* very much. . .I stay forever with my love. *Capisce*? One kiss. . ." A whiff of bacon wafted into the cabin from the kitchen. It was Elvira, belting out a horridly shrill song while preparing breakfast.

I wriggled my skeleton in an attempt to loosen the rope tied snug around me. It was to no avail. I kicked my leg bones up but couldn't free my ankle bones from the rope secured tightly around them.

"Drats. I'm caught."

Just then, Elvira waltzed in, carrying a plate of hot food. "*Buongiorno*! You are awake, *amore mio*! I have brought you some bacon and toast. You must be very hungry." She set the food down on the side table near the sectional. "Oh, I forgot! You can't use your arms."

I glared at her.

"Tsk-tsk. I will feed you breakfast!" She smiled and picked up a burnt piece of toast and shoved the entire slice into my mouth. I heard the concerning sounds of the hard-as-rock bread breaking apart, its sharp edges scraping painfully against the corners of my mandible.

All I could do was helplessly chew.

Then she picked up two pieces of charred bacon, dripping with grease, and crammed them into my mouth. Yuk! I wanted to spit out the slimy, rancid meat. She brought a glass of orange juice from the breakfast tray and held it against my mandible at an angle. The liquid spilled into my mouth nonstop, with most of it falling onto the carpeting in the cabin. Coughing and choking, I turned my skull away.

"Oh? You've had enough, *mi amore*?"

My shoulder bones drooped. I sighed, too defeated to ask this fanatic goth woman why she had tied me up. But she kept looking into my face with her heavily lidded eyes, encircled with thick black eyeliner, blinking, and smiling her black-lipstick smile.

I couldn't contain myself. A reaper could tolerate only so much. "Why did you tie me up?" I growled.

"Oh, *amore mio*, don't raise your voice at me. I have only wonderful things planned for us."

Us? "Like what?"

She smiled coyly, bringing her fingers up to her chin, and turning her body slightly. "You will see. But first, I must get you safely to our destination."

My brow bone shot up. "Where are you taking me?"

"Why, back to Italy, of course."

Italy? This goth nutcase kidnapped me and was now speeding me to an international destination? And she planned to take me across the rough Atlantic in this little boat? The furious ocean will rip it into smithereens, and I'll be on it!

I looked over her shoulder and out of the window. Hilly terrain toward the west was visible.

"There's land over there. You sure you're going the right way?"

"I'm going by way of the Caribbean, where there are fewer maritime law enforcement monitoring the seas to upset my plans."

On high alert, my spine straightened, as if I'd just grown an extra two inches. "Uh, what plan is that?" I dared ask this raving madwoman.

Elvira grazed her long pointy black fingernails across my shoulder bones, then over the breadth of my rib cage. She stooped to look me directly in the eye sockets and said in a thick, syrupy voice, "*Amore mio*, we are going to be married."

Instantly, my head spun. My bones felt weak. If I had eyeballs, they'd have rolled back in their sockets. I fell backward on the sofa and laid there until the early afternoon.

Upon rousing, Elvira still sang her nasally tunes and walked back and forth across the hull. I groaned, realizing the seriousness of my unusual predicament. A goth woman had plans to marry me in Italy, and I was helpless to do anything about it.

Clearly, Elvira heard my moans and popped her head into the cabin. "You are awake from your nap, *amore mio*!" she said, her voice chipper.

Here was my chance. "Uh, listen, Elvira, about the marriage thing. See, I have other plans. Besides, I'm not really the marrying kind, and—"

She stomped down the stairs and lunged her suddenly flushed face forward. "Shush! Don't dare speak such nonsense."

I stared at her. Two red horns seemed to grow from the top of her head. I swore I saw a red tail with a perfectly triangular end swish out from behind her and go back to hiding between her legs. Her nostrils flared, and puffs of gray smoke emanated from them.

As she stood with her hands on her hips, I shook my skull to clear it. I looked again.

This time, she wore a sunny black-lipstick smile, and she sat down next to me. "Pitiful Reaper," she started saying, while stroking my skull, surprisingly gently. "You understand so little. You don't see the wonders of marriage, of true love. Without me, you'd know nothing of the joys of togetherness."

I sat silent and still. Only my eye sockets followed her as she slowly got up and walked out of the cabin.

Sighing, it was hard to know what to do next. I couldn't do much, really. Not move my arm bones, not walk right off the boat—no matter how badly I wanted to. Basically, all I had the ability to do was sit on the sofa in the cabin and drown in self-pity. And that's what I did for the next several hours.

Darkness descended, which meant dinnertime. After breakfast, I wasn't looking forward to any further meals from her. Elvira's humming sounded louder. She approached the cabin. I watched her legs climb down the stairs. In her hand was a plate heaping with steaming food. Ugh, not again.

"*Amore mio*. Don't think I would miss giving you dinner." She shoved the plate into my face. "Here. Eat." Then she stepped back and laughed. "Oh, I forgot. You can't do anything without me."

She laughed louder and bigger this time. "But don't worry. I'm here to help you, my soon-to-be darling husband." Elvira chopped up the stuffed green peppers with rice into bite-size pieces. Then she pushed the food, heaping spoonful by spoonful, into my mouth. It was horrid, like noshing rotten vegetables and undercooked rice smothered in a sour tomato sauce that disguised the foul taste of the whole shebang.

She dabbed the corners of my mandible with a white cloth napkin. "There, there, all clean."

I couldn't believe the mess I was in. How did this even happen? I decided to take matters into my own hands. Surely, she could be swayed by reason. And she'd certainly appreciate candidness. What woman didn't?

"Elvira," I started to say with air of calm and confidence. "I've got to be honest. I don't really want to marry you. I'd appreciate if you could untie—"

She whipped around to glare at me in the tiny cramped cabin. She stood so close that her loose dark hair gave my face bones a painful whipping.

Her eyes grew big. Her nostrils widened, as if to inhale the powers of darkness in the, well, darkness. She pursed her lips until they almost disappeared into her fleshy, reddened face.

I figured a volcanic eruption was about to happen right before my eye sockets. I turned away to avoid watching the impending disaster unfold.

But all remained quiet.

Cautiously, I turned again, only to find Elvira smilingly cheerily.

"Reaper *innocente*," she said with a laugh and a clap of her hands. "You fail to understand the *bella vita*, a beautiful marriage. Do not fear. I promise to show you all that you've been missing." She waved the fingers on her left hand in front of my face, as if to say toodle-oo. Then she walked up the stairs.

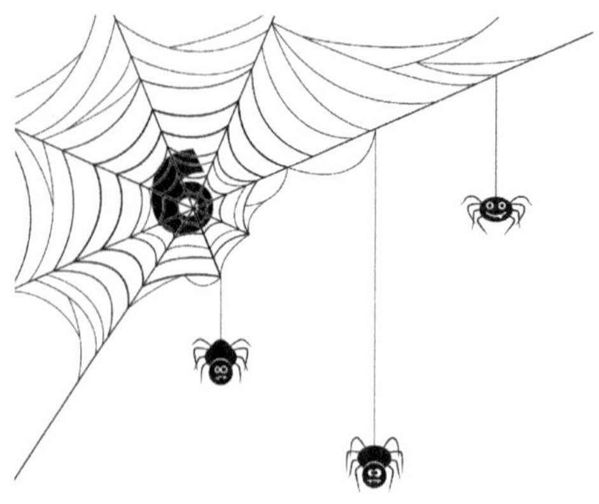

The hours turned into sordid days. The days turned into embittered weeks.

The boat sailed south, down the eastern coast, hugging Florida's shoreline, through the Gulf of Mexico, then along Central America's coastline. Luckily, we didn't encounter any off-season hurricanes or tropical storms. Strangely enough, I'd have welcomed either. An unforgiving hurricane would've thrown us off course and helped me make a clean escape from Elvira's fetters. I guess I wasn't so lucky.

Between steering the boat and poking her head into the cabin to feed me gross concoctions, Elvira was all achatter. My ear bones didn't get a rest.

She flopped down into the seat next to me and shoved a bridal magazine into my face bones. "Look at this black wedding gown on the cover, how *bella*. The black lace sleeves are gorgeous." She pointed at the tattooed fashion model wearing dark purple lipstick and a somber smile. "Oh, the black chiffon on this gown is so alluring!" She didn't stop there. "Mmm, Reaper, what do you think of a lacy black crop top wedding dress?" She looked at me. What was I supposed to say? Her muffin top couldn't be missed then? I thought it safer to stay quiet and sat as morose as a dead body.

"I wish I could sample the wedding cake before I order it," she complained and threw her hand on her forehead in a dramatic show. "Oh, oh, Reaper, look at this three-tiered black cake, with the black swirls, like spider webs, and the full black roses." She flipped the page. "Ooh, how about this cake with bloodred frosting and black icing dripping down it?" Her body quivered next to me, as if she were excited about masterminding a gruesome death scene. I couldn't help wondering about my safety.

"We mustn't forget the Italian priest! He'll officiate, dressed all in black. I'll order him to grow a dark beard too." She giggled like a child. "The place settings will be all black, with tall black candles and black chiffon decorating the dining tables. Over the plates will be placards, saying, 'Til Death Do Us Part.'" She turned to me. "I am picturing our wedding already and can't wait for it. Can you?"

How could I tell her that I wasn't the least bit interested and that, in fact, the best I could do was serve as lifelike decor for her marriage ceremony, which I wished didn't involve me in any way?

"What is a wedding without a honeymoon?" she asked, turning to me. "What do you think about Venice?" I opened my jaw, about to respond. Elvira instantly returned her attention to the glossy magazine and leaped headfirst into her rigmarole about the wonders of the City of Canals. Clasping her hands together, she said, "The gondolas are the symbols of romance! Plus, they are black! We shall ride all afternoon in San Polo, then during sunset in the quiet Campo San Barnaba, when it is most romantic."

I pictured myself trembling in the gondola, floating down the narrow canals with Elvira, the woman of my nightmares. Maybe the gondolier, in his black pants and striped shirt, would sing and drown out Elvira's incessant chatter. If not, I'd plead with him to help me escape from her grasp. But with my luck, he'd speak only Italian or a little German, neither of which I understood, and be of no use.

I sat there on the boat cushion, wallowing in my misery.

"But first, *amore*, where shall we get married?" She didn't wait for my answer. Instead, she pointed to a colorful photograph of rolling green hills on the pages of her wedding magazine. "Naples! Ah, it shall be so beautiful, with terraces and a lovely view of the Island of Capri. Ooh, look, it's so close to Vesuvius."

My brow ridge went up. Mount Vesuvius was still an active volcano and long overdue for an eruption. What were the chances it would spontaneously erupt on our, ahem, wedding day, gush with lava at two thousand degrees Fahrenheit, and cover us with suffocating, molten ash, leaving Elvira on my list of souls to pick up and me free of these unbearable shackles? I daydreamed of the glorious possibilities as she yapped on and on about the romantic atmosphere of the city and its famous Bay of Naples.

Curious as to what nonsense she'd bring up next, I peeked over at the open pages of her wedding magazine resting on her lap. Its photos seemed to inspire her about every facet of a marriage ceremony, including the exchange of rings. I'd never worn one, and I definitely wasn't about to wear a wedding ring.

"A diamond, Reaper, is rare, just as our love is rare. And so," she said, looking at me, "you shall place on my finger a 33-carat diamond wedding ring." She stretched out her left arm, eyeing and wiggling her ring finger. "The diamond ring will symbolize your eternal love for me." She pressed her hand against her, um, heart. "It will show everyone in Italy how much you love me!" She threw her arms in the air, as if in celebration of some romantic love that played out only inside her strange head.

"And the music. I need music for my bridal procession, something chilling." She glanced upward, as if beseeching the heavens, but clearly that realm wasn't waiting for her.

"I can hear it now. The creepy organ playing the wedding march, a little off-key, the cymbals crashing, the chorus singing. We must have a live chorus, and I'll insist they be headless."

What?

"Don't be afraid, *amore mio*." She must've noticed my skeleton break out in a tremble, because she gently patted my cloaked skull. "I mean the chorus will be costumed, appearing as if they're headless." She chuckled, somewhat coldly, sending shivers down my spine.

"Oh, I'll get to the music later. But first, we must set the wedding date!"

I groaned, silently, though, as this fiend was still sitting next to me. I didn't want to upset her moment of reverie planning her goth wedding—and jeopardize my well-being, which was under threat already.

She leaned over the sofa and to the side table. Pulling out the drawer, she reached for a small calendar. It was as if she'd known all along that she needed a calendar on her boat—a calendar to plan a wedding after kidnapping me. How long had she been planning this heist?

Elvira flipped through the months. "We shall set a date that is memorable, something neither of us would ever forget." She placed her palm over her heart, though I didn't believe she had one. "But how can either of us ever fail to remember the date our love officially begins?" She closed her eyes, as if dreaming. But I was in the clutches of a living nightmare.

"No, no, a Valentine's Day wedding is too far off. We cannot wait that long to begin our love." She continued flipping, then stopped at October and stared at the days. "*Amore mio*! Sweetest Day! It is perfect for our wedding." She drew a big red circle around the third Saturday of October. She stood up and looked at me. "We shall get married on Sweetest Day!"

"It is not too far off. Only a few months. I shall make the arrangements." Flicking her long straggly dark hair off her rounded shoulders, she turned and stomped up the stairs; I wish I could've said light as a bunny, but her stomping was more like an angry ogre on the verge of doing something terrible.

I sighed long, glad she was gone. Still tied up, I had nowhere to go. Sweetest Day, humph. The day struck me for some reason. "Sweetest Day," I kept repeating silently to myself, trying to jog my memory. My existence had been turned upside down lately, and thinking of anything else was difficult.

Then it hit me like a ton of bricks: I had promised to take Life out on a date on Sweetest Day! Ugh, I couldn't stay trapped in this dire circumstance. I had to find a way off this boat. Not only for myself but to take out the most gorgeous cosmic force in the universe! I couldn't let Life down, not then, not ever. I wouldn't miss this twice-in-an-eternity chance to be with the one creature who made my spine tingle, who made me smile even when situations demanded a frown and an ugly cry. Plus, I gave Death my word—and a reaper never went back on his word.

Gracious skeletons. How was I going to escape?

Elvira hurled curses on deck, threw her arms up, and kicked the bow.

Curious, I looked through the window. The boat wasn't chugging along as fast as it had been. In fact, it'd been sputtering and losing energy the past few miles. Elvira stomped her feet and curled her hands into fists so tight that the whites of her knuckles showed.

"Is anything the matter?" I yelled out to her from the cabin.

She plodded down the stairs, her face as red as a strawberry and her nostrils flared. "It's the old fuel tank. I should've known better than to use this aged boat for such an important voyage. Sediment is clogging the fuel filter." She clenched her fists in front of her chest and yelled into the stone-deaf sky, "It's ruining the engine!" She fussed so much that I couldn't imagine what her reaction would've been like under an actual life-threatening emergency.

"I need tape." She scanned the cabin, then yanked open all the drawers until she found a roll. "The fuel line just cracked too. It's stopping the gas from getting into the engine." Holding up the roll of masking tape she grumbled, "I'll tape it, but it's only a temporary fix."

My eye sockets widened. "What're you going to do?"

"I don't know yet," she muttered under her steaming breath.

I saw my chance. "Why don't you call the harbor master for help?"

She glowered at me. It was as if her eyes were two red-hot lasers piercing through my skeleton. "Oh? And have them conveniently dispatch the US Coast Guard?"

Which was just what I wanted. The Coast Guard would discover me tied up belowdecks and prosecute Elvira's criminal activities of kidnaping, holding me hostage, and trying to forcibly marry me. These triple federal and/or state offenses would've landed her in jail.

She went back up to tape the fuel line.

While she was up there, several boaters passed by. Seeing us stranded in the Gulf, they yelled out, asking if she wanted a tow. Elvira yelled back to each and every one of them in the cheeriest tone I'd heard from her all day, "Everything's fine. I'm just looking for a good fishing spot. The fish are biting this time of year!" Then she smiled her sunny black-lipstick smile and waved.

I dropped my jaw. The two-faced kidnapper could really put on a show.

Elvira was on deck for a few hours. The boat still hadn't moved much. I started to imagine it steadily sinking, with me still pathetically tied up and helpless. Swimming didn't come naturally to me. I had little reason to perfect my stroke. Ferrying souls to the next world kept me inside my boat, not struggling to stay afloat in the cold, deep, murky water.

Evening started to envelop the sky over the Gulf. Just before darkness descended, a brief flash of bright orange caught my attention. I peered through the slanted glass windows. Elvira was putting on a life jacket.

"The nerve!" My brow bones narrowed. Undoubtedly, the boat had more than one life vest, and she wasn't handing me one. If this boat sank, at least I'd float to the top wearing it, even with my arm bones tied up. At best, I could've bobbed up and down like a buoy in the water. Instead, she left me at the mercy of the sea! "Elvira. Typical," I muttered.

Out of nowhere, a splashing repeatedly sounded. "What in the afterworld is that?"

I pressed my face bones against the window glass and strained my eye sockets, trying to peer out into the foggy darkness, like an ethereal hellscape in which I was bound. It was difficult to see through the thick fog, but I made out a black blob at the side of the boat. It was furiously paddling the water with a ten-foot oar. I inched back, thinking I'd seen steam whooshing out of the top of the blob's head.

It was Elvira, so desperate to make her sinister plans work that she was fiercely paddling the boat under the cover of darkness and dense fog! Only insanity could drive this tormented woman to navigate at night, which distorted distances, and when obstacles and dangers were harder to see. Boats could've come out of nowhere, and, not noticing us, would've crashed, causing a gruesome mess in the open water. And how good was her hearing to detect foghorns and other boats approaching?

Trembling in my bones, I turned from the window. My insides flip-flopped chaotically. It was no telling what perilous circumstances this frantic woman would throw me into next.

A shackled reaper could do little. I laid my bones on the sofa and tried to sleep off my growing worries.

The morning sun rose, and I awoke to the sounds of splashing. Apparently, it'd gone on all night. I faintly recalled being roused about every half hour upon hearing the noises. I looked out of the window to see land in the distance. The boat steadily approached the shore.

Then loud curses filled the invigorating sea air. Without warning, Elvira trudged down the steps, into the cabin, still yelling profanities.

Her face was beet red, her shoulders drooped, and her rounded body was hunched over, as if she were ready to collapse from sheer exhaustion at any second.

"Buongiorno!" I greeted her, as chipper as I could muster, considering I'd been tied up and held hostage for weeks and didn't care to say hello to my captor. Plus, the last thing I needed was to be alone at sea with a crazy woman on the verge of going madder.

Her sharp gaze ripped my empty insides apart. Clearly, she'd worked herself up furiously paddling last night and was in no mood for niceties this morning.

"Saw you paddling," I said, trying to make conversation and lighten the morose vibe in the air.

Elvira just looked at me, glaring silently, as if plotting my doom—which she, unmistakably, already had.

"You know, I could've helped. I've got centuries' worth of experience paddling boats."

She ignored my selfless proposal.

"We're nearly there," she muttered, her every word loaded with vehement rage.

"Uh, nearly where?" We couldn't have reached Italy so soon.

"Puerto Viejo. A small village."

Costa Rica? We were headed to a tiny Central American country?

"That's a far cry from Italy," I said, wondering what she was up to.

She darted another angry look at me. "It's only a stopover. Until I fix my boat." Then, just as suddenly and strangely as a thunderous summer storm cleared to blue skies, she said with a grin that made my skeleton cringe, "Nothing's going to stop me from marrying my true love."

She disappeared up the stairs.

I grunted, then looked out of the window, only to be greeted by sandy beaches, coconut palms, and date palms swaying in the gentle sea breeze.

Seconds later, Elvira came back down carrying something fluffy and white in her hands.

"We're almost to the shore." She pushed the white item toward me. "Wear this."

"What is it? I'm not exactly free to put anything on." I nodded toward the rope tied around my arm bones.

She huffed. "I will help you."

She leaned down and draped the white cotton robe over my cloaked skeleton, arm bones and all, then stood back. "There, the rope is not visible."

I looked down at my new costume and asked, "Uh, we're heading to shore?"

"Of course. We're staying in a private villa. I made all the arrangements this morning."

She looked down at my ankle bones. "Tsk-tsk. You cannot walk like that." She clasped a metal chain from her waistbelt to the rope around my arms. Chained to her, I couldn't escape from her even on shore.

Then she brought out a pocketknife from her back pocket and sliced the rope at my ankle bones. It fell to the floor. "There, now you will follow me."

Elvira escorted me off the boat. We trudged through the shallow water, its slow, sharp-crested waves bashing against my femur bones, and toward the uninhabited shore. I looked back at the boat, bobbing up and down on the ripples of the shimmery blue sea.

"I'll go back to properly beach the boat once you're safe."

Safe? What did she mean by that?

As her prisoner, with my arm bones shackled to my sides and the white robe concealing my distressing condition, I stumbled onto the beach.

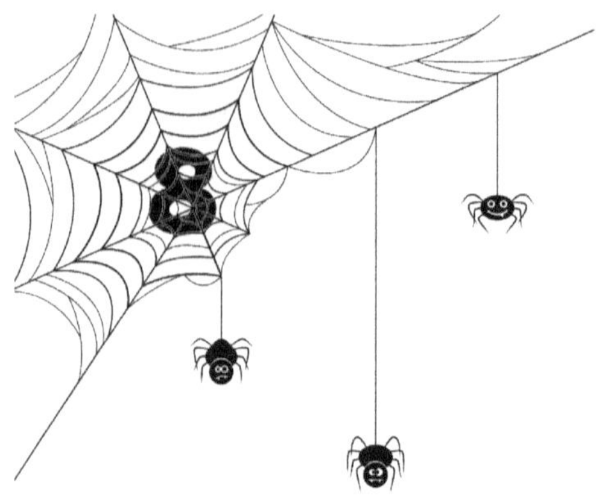

Elvira led me into her beachside villa on stilts. Palm mangroves secluded it in all directions, creating a natural fence, like around a high-security prison. It kept scheming trespassers out and freedom-loving residents in. The villa's exterior was painted a pomegranate red, and the ceilings were built out of bamboo stalks. Square windows formed a wall facing the beach. In fact, in place of the villa's interior walls were a series of clear glass windows.

We walked inside to a lime-green interior with glossy wooden door frames. This place must've been built in the seventies, when lime-green was in. The two-bedroom place came fully furnished, with plush white sofas, reclining armchairs, wooden side tables, and a dining table in the kitchen. I glanced out the back windows to see an aqua tile structure with steps leading up to the top.

"What's that?" I asked.

Elvira looked to where my gaze had stayed and replied, "It is the hot tub. We shall enjoy lovely afternoons together amid its bubbles."

I flung my skull back. There was no way I'd get into a hot tub with this hostage-taker.

Also in the backyard were lounge chairs, all flattened out and ready to be laid upon for an afternoon of sunbathing or briefly escaping the grips of a crazy kidnapper. The leaves of tall palm trees shaded the patio from the hot Caribbean sun.

"I can't wait to change into my swimsuit and jump into the pool," Elvira said, referring to the rich blue figure-eight-shaped pool beyond the hot tub.

No, no. I couldn't even look at her clothed. How was I going to manage seeing her prancing around in a bathing suit—unflattering as the sight of it promised to be?

I changed the subject quickly.

"So, when will the boat be fixed?" I asked.

"It will take time. The in-line fuel filter must be replaced, and fuel stabilizer must be added. I spoke with a boating repair service here and the delivery of the fuel filter will be delayed. Seems supply chain issues are holding up the delivery."

"I see. Uh, how long is the delay?" I asked, uncertain I wanted to hear the answer.

"A few months."

My eye sockets popped. A few months? Elvira was planning on holding me hostage in this two-story Costa Rican villa for a few months? I couldn't take it. Even worse, I was still chained to her side.

"You plan on keeping this chain on me?" I asked, nodding toward it.

She looked down at her waist. "Oh, *mio*. I forgot about it." She pulled out a small key from her cleavage and twisted it in the lock on the chain, liberating my skeleton from her.

But my arms were still tied, leaving me helpless.

Bound, I explored the rest of the villa with her, eyeing the cozy hammock hanging from the rafters. The drapes were open throughout the place, giving the villa an airy feel.

Walking upstairs, she pointed into a bedroom, fully furnished with a king-size canopy bed. "You'll sleep in there." She took the bedroom down the hall. "We're not married yet—but we will be soon!" She giggled.

Ah, a highly conservative kidnapper.

As I looked around at all the expensive, potted exotic ferns, the golden glow of the lights illuminating the fancy pool outside, and the man-made waterfall on the side of the villa, I wondered how loaded Elvira was. Where'd she get all this money from? She'd purchased this luxury villa on the spot for a few months' stay. She owned a boat and proudly had it named it after me. She didn't worry about a penny.

I considered going along with the wedding just for the lavish lifestyle Elvira afforded. I could simply cover my eye sockets whenever she entered the room. Tuning her out when she sang her nasally love songs was a practical solution. Pretending to enjoy her cooking and then secretly spitting the food out behind one of those pricey potted ferns was also doable. I could, after all, adjust to living with Elvira. It'd take some major rehauling on my part, but I'd have the sea to myself, go surfing, and hike the jungles.

I sighed.

But I couldn't bring myself to do it. I had more integrity than faking a relationship with a fanatic goth woman. I had to get myself out of this dire situation.

Elvira walked into the second-story living room. "Don't you just love it here?" She clasped her hands together in front of her chest. "The Caribbean air makes romance so easy." She darted her glance toward me. "Say you'll be mine, *amore mio*." She tilted her head and gave me her black-lipstick smile.

"Uh, no can do, senorita."

Her dark brows narrowed, her fists clenched, and her nostrils flared. I'd seen this expression before, and it didn't end pretty.

"You will be mine," she growled. At once, her tense shoulders relaxed and her fists loosened. She said with a spontaneous smile, "But it'll take time, *amore mio*. We have lots of it before our long-awaited wedding." She batted her long dark fake eyelashes.

I felt a bit nauseous and teetered on my feet bones.

"Oh, you seem unwell," Elvira said and pointed to a chair. "Sit down, *amore mio*."

I tottered over and sat my bones down. Elvira went down to the kitchen.

As I simmered in my misery, I remembered I had souls to pick up. Thank goodness that Earth time didn't match otherworldly time. But I still had to tend to my professional duties.

Elvira walked in from up the stairs, carrying a tray of two frosty glasses of lemonade with lemon slices on the sugared rims. "Here you are, *amore mio*."

I nodded toward my arm bones, still tied up. At the same time, I decided to speak up about my predicament.

"Listen, Elvira, I know you mean, ahem, well. But I can't stay tied up like this. I'm a professional, and I've got a job to do. My boss will come looking for me."

I wasn't sure if Death would send out a search squad for me, but he certainly wouldn't hesitate to express his displeasure if I lagged behind on my collections of souls. Most important, my personal work ethics kept me from leaving awaiting souls hanging in limbo, wondering where I was.

Elvira set down the tray on the coffee table.

"Well, I wouldn't want to stand in your way, would I?"

She brought out her penknife from her back pocket and began to cut me loose. Once unfettered, I shook my arm bones free, for the first time in weeks. Ah, liberation felt good. I threw my arms bones into the air, jiggled them, and brought them back down. I did this a few times, as Elvira looked at me strangely.

I was finally free of the restraints and eyed the front door through the upper-floor rails. I could just walk out and be free of Elvira too.

"Well, I'll be seeing ya," I said nonchalantly, and headed downstairs toward the door.

"I wouldn't do that if I were you." Her voice sounded at an unusually lower pitch and rather menacing, like some wretch who'd clambered up from the underworld.

My bones trembled. I slowly turned around to see her glowering at me, her beady black eyes laser-focused on my every move.

"I've got something you want."

Ha! What could she possibly have that I wanted?

Then she reached into her jiggling cleavage and pulled out a silver dog tag.

My jaw dropped.

She dangled the dog tag in front of her face. "You'll want this, eh, *amore mio*?"

It was my precious titanium dog tag engraved with a photo of Life and me on Valentine's Day, the first time I took her out. I remembered asking Life for a selfie of us that evening, then I had it engraved on a dog tag the next day. No one in the universe but me knew I had that photo of us. I'd always kept it tucked in my inner cloak pocket and only brought it out when I needed a little cheer to brighten my day. That dog tag held my only photo of Life and me together—and Elvira had it in her clutches!

The fiend must've searched through all my cloak pockets when she gave me the laced drink that knocked me out on her boat.

"And this!" Elvira reached farther into her cleavage and pulled out my phone.

I couldn't call for help without my phone.

A reaper my size didn't have to tolerate this nonsense. I'd just grab my dog tag and phone from her hands and be on my merry way. Nothing was stopping me.

As I ambled toward her, she stepped back and dangled her arm out of the open second-story window.

"One more step, and your precious dog tag and phone will drop into the tide pool below." She squinted her eyes, gleaming with evil, and smiled wickedly, made doubly wicked by her midnight-black lipstick.

I stopped dead in my tracks. If she dropped my dog tag into the tide pool, I'd never find it. The pocket of seawater would've washed it into the Caribbean by the time I ran to the ground floor. A phone was replaceable but not my only beautiful photo of Life and me on Valentine's Day. It was priceless.

"No, no. Don't do it. I'll stay," I assured her repeatedly, pushing my hand bones in front of me.

Elvira brought her arm inside and tucked my possessions into her cleavage again.

"You'll go to work, and you'll return to me, every single day, if you want to see your beloved dog tag again." Her vacant stare cut through my skeleton.

My shoulder bones drooped, and my gaze fell to the floor. My skull hung the lowest it'd been in my seven-hundred-plus-year existence. All the oxygen in my rib cage drifted out as a I released a long, deep sigh.

"Okay."

Bright and early the next morning, I hopped down the stairs to the kitchen nook. Elvira stood at the stove, frying pancakes. At least, at first glance, they looked like pancakes. I anticipated sweet golden syrup, a thick pad of butter on my plate—the full works to disguise Elvira's horrid cooking.

"*Amore mio*! Would you like some frico, Italian potato pancakes, with a topping of recycled cheese?"

I took a look into the frying pan with an inch of oil sputtering inside its rim and considered her offering of recycled foodstuffs. "Uh, I'm not really hungry."

"Tsk-tsk. The Parmesan cheese rinds have just been recycled. You are missing out!" she said with her black-lipstick smile, as she maneuvered the slotted spatula over the food crisping in the hot oil then inverted the sizzling, browned frico onto a ten-inch plate.

“I will be going out shopping today. Right after I have a nibble of breakfast. I have much to buy.”

Seeing an opportunity, my brow bone arched. “Oh? Well, while you’re out, I’ll clean up the place. You know, since we’ll be staying here a while. We might as well reside in a villa that’s neat and tidy.”

She switched off the gas burner and turned to me with a jubilant smile. “*Amore mio*! I knew you’d come around. Love works in mysterious ways!” she exclaimed, clasping her hands in front of her chest.

Immediately, she turned to a cabinet door behind her, opened it, and pulled out a white cloth rolled into a tiny ball. She pushed it into my empty abdominal cavity. “Here, wear this.”

I unfolded the cloth. It was a little lacy white waist apron. “Uh, sure. This’ll go great with my cloak.” Hesitantly, I tied the apron over my cloak, around my waist.

Then Elvira dug her arm into the cabinet again and pulled out a feather duster. “Here,” she said, shoving it into my hand bones.

“Yeah, I sure could use this. It’ll certainly, uh, help as I clean.”

She clapped her hands together, took a few bites of her frico, and rushed out the door. “See you soon, my love!” The door closed.

I breathed a sigh.

I looked around the place. Two whole floors awaited me. I'd tackle the upstairs first, then work my way down to the second floor. This couldn't be too difficult. In fact, I anticipated being done in a jiffy.

Grabbing my feather duster, I walked up the steps to the second floor. The windows remained opened wide, ushering in the cool sea breeze throughout the entire upper level.

Elvira's bedroom was a good place to start. Her bedroom windows gave panoramic views of the Caribbean Sea in three directions. A small ceiling fan twirled, circulating the fresh air. Her queen-size bed was neatly made with a fluffy white comforter on top. The room was pretty sparse, considering most of the luxuries lay in the breathtaking views of the never-ending sea.

I waltzed in, thinking it'd be a no-brainer. She kept whatever was valuable there, after all. I dusted the small nightstand and the top of the gleaming cherrywood dresser. All the while, I opened the drawers and rummaged through them.

"Come on, it's got to be here," I mumbled to myself, pushing aside the half-used notepads, cheap earrings with their fake gold chipped off, and the crumpled Kleenex. But it wasn't.

I opened her double closet doors, finding plush red-and-orange beach towels hanging on the wooden hangers.

I searched through the interior, not finding what I was looking for.

"It must be downstairs."

I hurried down the steps and began in the kitchen. The contents of not a single drawer or cupboard escaped my hawk-eyed attentiveness. I turned over every pot and pan, ran my finger bones over all the steel utensils, and dug my arm bone deep into the farthest recesses of the pantry. Still, my hunt proved fruitless.

It'd been two hours, and I came up empty-handed.

"The living room!" Racing to the other side of the villa, bathed in bright daylight, I pulled out the couch and recliner cushions. "Humph, nothing here." Upon turning over the wicker foot rests, I found the undersides empty.

A series of ornate paintings of the orange Caribbean sunset hung in a cluster on the walls. "Surely, she must've hidden it behind the artwork. They're the perfect hiding spots. Not even a burglar would think to look there." I rushed to the far wall, plucked each of the three colorful paintings one by one off their metal hooks, and investigated behind them. The spaces were clear as a summer day.

Then I remembered the pricey ferns in the corner of the room. "Those are the last hiding places in the entire villa. If my dog tag isn't in there, I don't know where else to look." My anticipation mounted. I'd be at my wits end if I failed, doomed to months of sheer agony with the gothic kidnapping temptress.

I scrambled toward the plants, disregarding the leaves, which must've taken decades to grow, and yanked the greenery out of their pots. Soil fell in a mess over the floor. "Drats. I'll have to clean that up."

Just as I spoke, the front door key jiggled in the lock. Elvira entered a moment later, carrying bags and bags filled with brand-new clothes overflowing from the tops.

She lowered her sunglasses down her nose and peered out over them at me.

"Uh, he-he, I was just polishing the leaves. You know, I wouldn't want to miss a single dust particle. We deserve to stay in the cleanest villa possible. Nothing beats a clean home." I gave her a sparkling grin.

She smiled. "*Amore mio*, you are too good, polishing the plants too!"

Upon dropping her bulky shopping bags to the floor, she pulled out a black two-piece bikini printed with large white skull bones and equally large white butterflies. "How do you like it?" she asked, holding it up.

"Uh, it's so you."

She pranced to the bathroom. At once, it occurred to me that she may have my dog tags on her person.

A second later she emerged wearing the skimpy thing.

Not wanting nightmares that night, I turned away, pretending to focus on polishing the dainty green fern leaves to a sheen.

In her goth swimwear, Elvira strolled across the living room, opened the patio door, and said, "I'm going for a swim, *amore*!"

She jumped into the pool, cannonball style, splashing water so far that it drenched my cloak from my hood to my hem as I stood with my gaping jaw in the middle of the living room. Wearing that horrendously little bikini, it was clear she wasn't hiding my dog tags on her.

Soaking wet, I dropped my skull. My dog tag was nowhere to be found, not in the villa, not in Elvira's cleavage. What was I to do? That once-in-an-eternity photo of Life and me was the only thing tethering me here. I couldn't leave until I found it.

Suddenly, the tinkling of a bell rang through the air. I looked around. The jingling came from near the pool. It was Elvira, ringing a tiny brass bell as she lounged on a beach chair poolside. She rang the bell nonstop. The constant, high-pitched jangle was cacophonous to my ear bones. I placed my hand bones over them. Still, I couldn't drown out the jarring sounds of her ringing the bell.

I stomped outside. "Do you need something?"

She set down the bell on the concrete patio below. "Amore mio, yes, I'd like a glass of lemonade." She pushed her sunglasses back up her nose and looked out over the water.

I blurted out, "Of course," and hurried inside.

Wait a minute. What just happened? I stopped dead in my tracks, realizing Elvira had just summoned me to serve her a drink poolside, as if I were her personal waiter in a sultry Caribbean resort eager to fulfill her every bidding and make her stay glorious.

What a hapless mess I found myself tangled up in!

Groaning audibly, I stomped to the fridge, pulled out the frosty pitcher with floating mint leaves and round lemon slices, and poured her a cold drink. I couldn't escape this nightmare, not without the dog tag back in my cloak pocket. With my vertebrae hunched over, I plodded to the poolside and delivered her beverage with a dainty pink drink umbrella.

Without my phone, I couldn't check my schedule for upcoming soul pickups. Death nowadays sent my schedule as a text attachment. It was far more convenient to receive it digitally than it was to head all the way to the office just to retrieve my latest schedule. Since it was continually updated with new souls needing to be collected, I had to have the most updated list at any given time.

This meant I was forced to go to the office and face my boss. Fortunately, or perhaps unfortunately, Elvira gave me permission to go to work, provided I return to her afterward.

Grunting, I made my way to the office. During my commute, I rehearsed what I'd tell Death. I couldn't possibly tell him a goth woman was holding me and my phone hostage. He'd be furious. My work phone held important private data, like the names of souls, their precise date and time of collection, and their phone number, which was a recently added bit of info, to accommodate my new habit of sending pre-pickup text messages—a new-and-improved way to make today's fetching of souls a lovely experience for everyone all around.

Death would be enraged to know I was no longer in possession of my phone. How could I face him in his unabashed fury? I looked up through the corners of my eye sockets, picturing him: the whites of his eyes turning red as the blood vessels burst, his dark, bushy eyebrows bouncing and furrowing and producing a mean glower, and the fearsome sounds of his vehement yelling that made my skeleton shudder.

I jumped back at the sight of it in my mind's eye socket.

Besides, Death was incredibly powerful and could do almost anything he wanted. He might send out a determined crew to investigate and track down my phone, even in places as far away as Costa Rica. Death had access to the entire world, after all. It was a task the crew would surely be successful at, since the boss hired only top-tier security.

He'd never believe Elvira wasn't interested in hacking the phone but only in shamelessly holding it as collateral for my hand bone in marriage. Caught in the act, she'd frantically attempt to defend herself and her sinister plans, going so far as to show them my dog tag with the photo of

Life and me together. Death would get wind of the photo—and Life too.

I couldn't show my face bones to Life if my true feelings were made as bare as an armadillo without its armor shell. I'd feel as naked as the nocturnal forager with a cougar hunting me, ready to flip me over and make a meal out of me. She'd never see me in the same innocent way again. It wouldn't be farfetched to imagine she'd dart the other way every time we crossed paths in the office. Would she even feel comfortable swapping dinner recipes if she were to know? And what about me taking her out on Sweetest Day? She'd never dance as freely in my arms. Death wouldn't even trust me.

The big boss was another story altogether.

Trembling, I dared picture his response: "What're you doing with a photo of *my* gal engraved on your dog tag?" he'd thunder.

It was a question that demanded a satisfying answer I couldn't provide. Was I supposed to say, "I've got a longtime crush on the love of your existence. I can't wait to take her out on Sweetest Day. She means the next world to me. I understand Life's your better half, but in the event that you lose interest, I'd be happy to—"

I wriggled my face bones. First off, Death couldn't exist without Life, and vice versa. Who was I but a lowly reaper in the service of one of the most powerful forces in the known universe?

No way could I have been candid with Death. He was my boss, and I was reaper crazy over his gal. It wasn't all too far-off to imagine myself getting the boot, being kicked out of my centuries-long position, and forced out into the terrifying limbo, the lonesome, dark and muddling in-between place where neither Life nor Death existed. I'd drift hopelessly in the empty nothingness for eternity, without a job, without purpose, without another jubilant moment with Life herself ever again.

Thinking about it gave me the shudders. No, I couldn't tell him. It was too great a risk, one I refused to take. Instead, I planned to fudge the truth—but it came out as an outright lie.

I knocked twice on Death's door.

"Come in."

I poked my skull through the crack. "Hey, boss. Do you have a minute? I won't take up much of your time. I've got a teensy issue. No biggie, really. Nothing to worry about."

"What is it?" Death asked, looking up from his desk, cluttered with pastel-colored sticky notes, a matching set of wire mesh organizers, and a miscellaneous assortment of old-fashioned office junk. Though the office was transitioning toward digital, some things were too practical for change.

Putting one foot bone inside, then squeezing myself through the door I'd cracked slightly open, my skeleton mostly entered his office. I kept one foot bone outside the door, an instinctual choice that'd have been useful in the event things went south and I had to run.

"I've got a minor request. I was hoping you could send me paper schedules, indefinitely."

Death's eyebrow arched as he gazed at me with concern. "Oh? Is there suddenly something wrong with texting it?"

I waved my hand bone in front of me and gave a little fake laugh. "No, it's nothing, really. I just have a longing to go back to the good ol' days, just for a bit. That's all." I smiled. "You know how it is when I've been doing my job one way for seven hundred years, and then I switch it up a bit. It's just me wanting to reminisce a little." I squeezed my index finger bone and thumb bone in front of my eye sockets.

"Well, all right."

He sounded unsure.

"Just let me know when you want to go back to me texting the schedule."

He didn't press me any further.

I breathed a sigh. "Thanks, boss. I hope it'll be soon, really soon."

He looked down to resume his paperwork.

From the out bin on the corner of his desk, I grabbed my current paper schedule, which he'd normally have scanned and texted me as an attachment.

Giving him a quick full grin, I closed the door.

Souls awaited me, so I ventured out to perform my shift. When my clients were ready for pickup, their souls lingered in the in-between realm, which meant I traveled to that dark, cocoon-like space to officially send them off to the next world. On the contrary, spending time in the earthly world required that I moved about as Earthlings did—via physical means, like, unfortunately, Elvira's boat. This meant I couldn't simply vanish, even when attempting to escape Elvira's clutches.

Collecting my clients took a different turn this time around. I didn't have access to my phone, so I couldn't send pre-pickup texts to alert souls of my impending arrival, as I'd done lately. By no means did this go unnoticed.

Chen, a skateboarder from Northern California, was due for a pickup. I arrived at the lake, where he teetered on his skateboard over the edge of the half-pipe built just beyond the banks of the water. The twenty-one-year-old dropped onto the ramp. By the visible lack of control of his board, this was clearly one of his first times dropping in from the top of the notoriously steep ramp.

He wore protective equipment, but it didn't stop me from swooping down just as his fall technique failed him. Chen didn't need hospitalization. He was too far gone and required my services right away.

“Hey, man, what’re you doing here?” Chen asked, wide-eyed and in a slight daze from his crash to the hard bottom of the pipe.

“I’m here to pick up your soul. What else?”

“Man, word is out on the streets that you text. How come you didn’t text me to say you was comin’?”

I dropped my gaze to the ground. My face bones turned pink as a flamingo. What could I say? That a crazy goth woman was holding my phone hostage? How did that reflect on me? I was a foreboding phantom, at a respectable seven-centuries-old, from the mysterious other side—and I couldn’t defend myself from a fanatic temptress. A sudden emasculating feeling turned my knee bones to Jell-O.

“Eh, you know how it is with phones. I’ve got tech issues.”

“Okay, man. But I wish I could’ve bragged to my friends that I got a text from the one-and-only Grim Reaper. You totally stole my thrill.”

I knew how he felt.

He got into the boat, and I ferried him through the deep, murky water safely to the other side.

Every client since blatantly complained about not receiving a pre-collection text from me. Some had even expressed their dismay at not reading my words of comfort and how my solace would’ve made their journey less frightful. After all, they shared that their friends or family in prior months had all received pre-pickup texts from me before their final departures to the next realm.

I couldn't blame them. I missed sending my texts too. I longed for the instant connection, establishing a meaningful rapport between myself and my end clients, a perk I'd only recently discovered once I got my first work phone. And already it was gone.

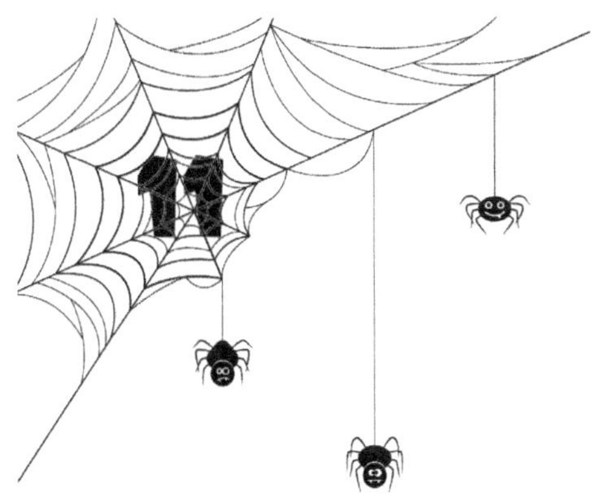

Elvira insisted we go out shopping. "There's so much to buy, *amore mio*!" She grabbed my arm bone and dragged me to the souvenir shops, their shelves stacked from top to bottom with bottles of the flavorful hot sauces that were staples in the homes of locals, tricolor carved wooden bowls, wooden toucans painted in the region's tropical colors, and bags and bags of coffee. In every direction I looked, bags of Arabica coffee packed the shelves. I was silently drawn to the coffee bags with the logo of a lounging skeleton across the front; it sort of spoke to me. Apparently, Costa Rica was a haven for coffee.

As if she were preparing to enter an underground bunker upon the threat of a world war, she grabbed all the five-pound bags of Villalobos, Catuai, Typica, Caturra, and Villa Sarchi coffee varieties her greedy hands could handle and threw them into the shopping cart, producing loud thuds. Upon finalizing the purchases, she shoved the weighty shopping bags into my arm bones for me to haul during the rest of the afternoon. Carrying seventy-five pounds of coffee beans was no small feat, especially as the tropical sun beat down on my bones and more shopping bags were constantly added to my duties.

Next, she yanked me by the cloak toward the artisan market selling handmade jewelry. I went along, no longer seeing the point in resisting. We were met with table upon table, blanketed in black cloth, over which laid turquoise jewelry, hand-crafted beaded necklaces, and brown leather bracelets. The tables were awash with specks of red, blue, silver, and orange hues.

"*Amore*, look at all the bamboo jewelry," Elvira shrieked, pointing. "Ooh, and the belly chains inspired by the ocean!" She first tried on the bracelets with a single seashell, then the sea glass earrings, the black mandala necklaces, and finally the boho belly chains dangling with charms. She held up a mirror the vendor had lent her to admire herself dripping head-to-toe in artisan jewelry.

"I'll take them all," Elvira said to the vendor, who beamed at having made probably the biggest sale ever.

Then she pulled me to the circular racks of clothing spinning in the Caribbean breeze. The tiny shops were another feast for the eye sockets. The bright reds, oranges, and blues popped. Tourists took photographs of each other smiling and holding up their pastel pink retail bags, as if they'd just won a medal for the best shopping spree. Actually, Elvira would've taken home the gold.

As Elvira browsed, her oversize purse dangled off my forearm bone. I waited as patiently as I could, which was pretty patiently, considering I had eons of experience waiting for dilly-dallying souls to make their final exits. Beads of sweat formed on my bones as I carried her gargantuan shopping bags loaded with brand-new clothing and more plush beach towels.

"Uh, excuse me, Elvira, but I can't help asking. Don't you have enough towels already?" I dared ask.

She spun her head around, as if I'd interrupted her moment of shopping bliss, and snapped back. "Don't order me around." Then a sunny smile appeared on her face that immediately wiped away her scowl. "I'd never order you around, *amore mio*." She blinked, then resumed her fervent browsing.

She rummaged through the wide assortment of bikinis, sarongs, and bamboo clothing. As if drawn by an irresistible magnetic force, she made an automatic beeline for the black bikini tops and bottoms and black sarongs.

Holding a teensy black bikini in front of herself, she asked, "How does it look?"

"Black is definitely your color," I replied, glad she didn't try them on and then pose her question, which would've probably caused me an instant second death.

We went shopping in the rest of the colorful markets, from the little outside vendors selling handsewn bags on the sandy beaches with sweeping views of the tree-filled mountains, to the grand air-conditioned malls with fancy escalators and perfectly manicured palm trees growing upward from the floor tiles. We visited the flea markets, the central markets, and the municipal crafts markets.

Elvira might as well have bought the whole country, because she loaded up my arms with bags upon bags of stuff, wiping the shelves clean of cheap and expensive products that landed in the bags on my arm bones. Carrying the overbearing weight of the goods all day, the curve of my spine deepened. Though the seawater surrounded us to the east, I grew dehydrated and nearly collapsed, logging her heavy purchases under the merciless rays of the sultry Caribbean sun.

"Do you mind if we rest?" I asked her.

Elvira darted her beady eyes at me and growled, "We have too much to do and see. We're here only a short time." She looked down at the bags in my hand bones. "And don't let the bags drag. You're getting them dirty."

"Yes, Elvira," I replied, dropping my gaze to the ground and lifting my arm bones, which ached.

She took me on a food walking tour, which I couldn't stomach, not in the fine company I was in. But she devoured the farm-to-table snacks and entrées faster than I could do a double take. The waterfall and coffee tour was tolerable, and would've been fantastic if it weren't for Elvira by my side.

All the shops bustled with laid-back shoppers. Tourists with white sunscreen on their glistening noses snapped selfies in their floral Hawaiian shirts. Locals wandered about leisurely looking for a tasty morsel to munch on. But I couldn't stop my nerves from rattling.

As our day of shopping turned to months of hitting the markets, it became clear that Elvira's pockets had no bottom. She was filthy rich. This meant only one thing: she'd continue her mindless habit of shopping every single day with me in tow. The more stuff that accumulated in the villa, the harder it was to find the one thing keeping me in Costa Rica—my dog tag.

After endless excursions to the shops and with no clue as to the whereabouts of my dog tag, a gradual hopelessness started to consume every bone in my skeleton. It became a routine: in between my professional rounds, I accompanied Elvira to the markets with my shoulder bones drooping and my skull hung as low as the full moon during a summer solstice.

Strangely, I started to anticipate the daily shopping events. I looked forward to dragging my skeleton up by six o'clock when the markets first opened and sweating and huffing upon carrying her shopping bags full of trinkets. She screamed at me and ordered me to do her bidding, but I didn't even cringe anymore. In the rare instance she bought me a bamboo pendant necklace, I interpreted her gesture as an overwhelming kindness, ignoring the fact that she insisted the pendant hold a photograph of her.

I went along with the daily activities: shopping and trips to the jungle, where I sat hunched over with Elvira as we watched sloths climb trees.

"Look how they go!" she exclaimed, her eyes sparkling as she slapped her palms against her cheeks.

I sat listlessly and watched the exciting event unfurl in front of my eye sockets: a three-toed sloth moving inch by inch up the ficus tree.

"How, um, riveting," was all I could muster, my voice as monotone as a white picket fence.

It occurred to me I had no better way to spend my evenings than watching a sloth climb precisely one foot up the tree trunk every ten seconds. In a single minute, the sloth had climbed six feet. By three minutes, the animal lounged in the treetops, only for Elvira to say, "Look, another sloth!" And the entire spellbinding observation process began all over again.

On the jungle rocks with Elvira peering through binoculars, I sat huddled, still as night, as hairy tarantulas crawled over my frayed cloak and mosquitoes buzzed near my ear bones. Nothing beat the experience of being at the mercy of the untamed jungle with my captor and a host of nighttime creepy-crawlers.

I gradually started to become aware of developing warm feelings for Elvira. Somehow, my bond with her increased my safety. If I obeyed her commands, I wouldn't be viciously screamed at. And, she let me go to work, which kept me from losing my mind entirely. Unless, I was already out of my mind and didn't know—it was hard to tell as the days and months blurred together with no hope in sight.

Ignoring my true feelings, which I believe had vanished somewhere into the bottom recesses of my skeleton, I flashed Elvira a big grin every time she demanded we visit the markets at 6:00 a.m., sit in the jungle amid terrifying vermin, or watch the locals perform traditional folkloric dances in their frilly, eye-catching white, red, and blue dresses as she stuffed her face with cheesy empanadas.

It was as if I'd lost myself in this luckless hostage situation.

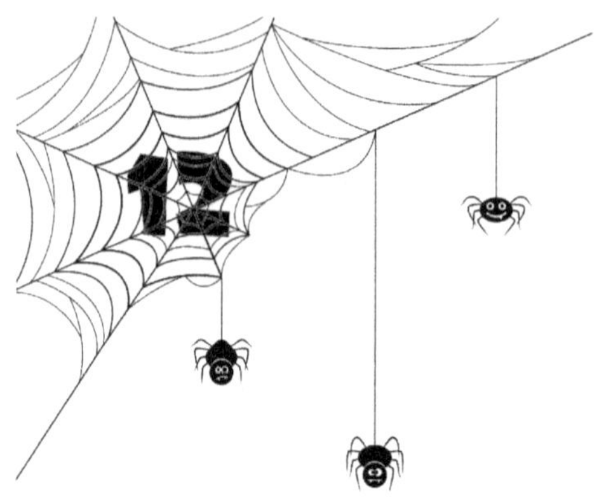

It was August already. The openness of the sea beckoned me, so I grabbed a beach towel and headed for the shore. As I sat on the sand, digging my toe bones deep into it, I gazed out across the water, extending for miles, wondering how long I'd be stuck in Costa Rica, in Elvira's suffocating grasp. No one could know about my secret crush on Life. I couldn't just up and run, because Elvira had the goods—my dog tag—to blackmail me to stay. And Sweetest Day was coming up in a couple months, when I agreed to take Life out for a good time. How was I going to manage that? It'd take nothing less than a miracle.

Not knowing what to do, I scanned the clear blue water and the lush tropical green jungle embracing the shoreline. It was like sitting in a refuge, safe from storms, wild animals, and Elvira, back in the villa.

It was a gorgeous spot to catch a wave and clear my skull.

I'd seen an old yellow surfboard lying against the side of the villa. Why not? I'd never surfed before, and Puerto Viejo was a popular surfing village. I was destined to ride the waves. The locals had talked about Salsa Brava, the most intense wave in the region. They'd said the torrid water was only for true surfers. Eh, how hard could it be? I'd seen tons of people plant their bare feet on their boards and ride the waves as if they owned the sea. Granted, I'd collected a number of souls on various oceans, but, in my hopeless circumstances, I had nothing to lose.

Invigorated by the purifying sea air and the soothing water, I ran to get the surfboard.

The smaller waves rolled to the edges of my feet bones. My eye sockets caught a powerful wave approaching. I climbed onto my board and paddled on my abdominal cavity farther out into the water.

I arched my spine and hopped onto the board as the superfast wave barreled toward me. The sea lunged against me and soaked my cloak, sending its tatters fluttering. My foot bones still clung to the board. I was a mere speck in the sea, yet I harnessed the unlimited power of the wave. I grew a bit cocky, as the board was mine to control. Feeling ambitious, I experimented with an aerial maneuver. On my board, I went up the wave vertically, reached the top, rotated my skeleton, then threw my arms out horizontally.

The adrenaline rush pummeled through my bones, overloading my senses. I felt the speed of the water, the wind against my face bones. The massive wave was powerful, and I was its humble passenger.

Then the nose of my board came down first. Something went wrong. I landed on the back of the wave and straightened my leg bones, not making the landing. I felt a sudden, shooting pain.

“My ankle bone!” I yelled and crashed into the water. The powerful Salsa Brava had broken it, like a twig. My first attempt at surfing proved to be injurious. The locals were right; the most intense wave in Costa Rica was for the pros. I needed to somehow get back to shore.

Swimming wasn’t a requirement for ferrying souls to the other side, so I never did it well, especially not with only one foot bone functional. Fortunately, my left ankle bone was leashed to my surfboard, which gave me buoyancy. I climbed onto the board and held on, as the wave pushed me to shore.

Hobbling on my left leg bone, leaning on my surfboard, and using it as a makeshift crutch, I inched my way across the beach, back to the villa. All the while, my right ankle throbbed and pulsed. Sharp pains tore through my leg bone and up toward my knee bone. I lost my balance amid the ache and accidentally put weight on it, causing an agony that left me writhing and screaming like a baby.

I reached the hammock swinging on the back porch and collapsed into it. My left leg bone hung out of the hammock, and my broken ankle bone rested, cradled inside it.

I must've slept for hours, because Elvira came out screaming, "Where have you been?"

My skeleton nearly jumped out of the hammock at the piercing shrillness of her voice. Instead, I pointed to my broken ankle and said, "It's fractured. I can't walk on it."

She looked down at my bruised ankle bone. "Oh, look, a crack. And part of your bone is shifted out of place." Immediately, a smile spread over her face. "Tsk-tsk. I'll take care of you, *amore mio*. It's a shame you cannot go anywhere."

I gulped.

Over the next two weeks, Elvira propped up my ankle bone on fluffy white pillows stacked one on top of the other on the bed. The down pillows added welcoming softness as my bone rested on them. She opened the curtains and windows wide, letting in the warm sunlight and refreshing Caribbean breeze.

"It must remain elevated," she said, pointing to my broken ankle bone.

She brought ice from her ice maker in the kitchen, put the cubes in a cloth bag, and covered my ankle bone with the cold compress. Icing my ankle bone reduced the pain, and the instant relief was all I could have asked for at that moment.

Three times per day, she brought in a plate of food: frico for breakfast, gnocchi or risotto topped with freshly grated Parmesan and a side of fish for lunch, and salad, soup, and meat for dinner. At every meal, I ate a forkful in front of her and said with a smile, "Delicious." When she left the room, I spat it out on the other side of the bed and tossed the rest of the food out the open window nearby.

"Yuk. How does anyone manage to consistently cook so terribly?" I asked myself.

I looked down at my broken bone. It hadn't yet healed. A broken bone could take weeks or months to improve, and I didn't have that kind of time. But Elvira showed incredible kindness to me. I couldn't believe the level of care she delivered. It came as a total shock, a one-hundred-eighty-degree turn from the seductive sea snake I'd known her to be, first on the boat, then here in Costa Rica.

One sunny day, she came in the room carrying a hand-carved wooden serving tray, an exotic-looking piece. On its center sat a bowl of minestrone soup, floating with beans, onions, pasta, and meat. I asked her to sit down. She did and set the solid wood tray on the foot of the bed.

"Elvira, you're being so good to me," I said, my empty chest cavity brimming with gratitude.

She inhaled deeply and gave me a warm, motherly smile. Her face seemed to glow a little, almost as if with genuine affection. She tilted her head and replied in the softest, most feminine voice I'd ever heard from her, "You must get well, *amore mio*."

She patted my skull.

"You're being so compassionate," I told her, my eye cavities gazing into her face.

She simply nodded. "The supplies for the boat are arriving soon."

"They're on their way?" I asked her, sitting up slightly.

"Yes, *amore mio*. Once the supplies come, the boat will be fixed shortly afterward."

"Uh-huh."

"Then we go to Italy."

I dropped my skeleton back on the bed.

"But don't worry."

My ear bones perked up. Maybe she would let me go. After all, she'd become so softhearted the past two weeks. Something in her might've changed and she came to her senses. I'd seen it before. Fiends did transform into angels in a twinkling.

"You will be better soon. You must get better. I insist."

"You're looking out for me," I said, looking up at her with a weak smile.

"Of course. I am looking out for us. If you do not get well, you cannot stand with me before the priest, at the altar, during our marriage ceremony." She suddenly stood up from the edge of the bed and scolded me. "How will it look if you limp during our wedding? It will be horrendous. You will make a scene!"

My jaw dropped. I felt the white color go out of my face bones.

She immediately sat down and stroked my skull again, all the while saying in the gentlest tone, "*Amore mio*, you know so little of the world, and especially of what love is. Don't worry, once we are married, I will show you true love."

I dropped my mandible to my chest bones.

"What is it, *amore mio*? You don't know if you will be well enough for our wedding?"

"I-I-I hope to get better soon." It was all I could muster as a heavy weight of worry mixed with mind-bending dread fell on my chest bones.

"*Amore*, say you'll be mine."

She looked into my face bones with her jet-black eyes, lined like that of a rabid raccoon, and flapped her dark eyelashes.

I swallowed hard.

But I couldn't fib, not now, not here. "Elvira, you've been remarkably caring these past two weeks."

She stared into my eye sockets with her black eyes.

"You've really shown me the gentler side of you."

Her chest heaved up and down.

"I'm really filled with appreciation that you're tending to me as I lay here. But—"

A flicker, like a tiny bolt of lightning, appeared in the corner of her dark eyes.

"But I can't say I'll be yours. It's just not possib—"

Elvira's nostrils flared. She pursed her lips. She shot up, grabbed the heavy wooden serving tray from the edge of the bed, and smashed it against my broken ankle bone. The soup bowl shattered, hurling shards of razor-sharp porcelain into my skeleton and over the bed. The glass tumbler fell to the floor and broke into a thousand pieces. Even the bright sun quickly hid behind gray clouds moving across the sky.

"Owww!" I yelled over and over in agonizing pain.

She marched to the door, spun around, and glared at my helpless, broken skeleton. She growled, "You *will* say you'll be mine on our wedding day." Then the heartless brute stomped off.

If pain could be a motivator for me to escape my distress, this was it.

Early the next morning, I swung my good and bad leg bones out of bed, which had supported me through the muggy night. Leaning on a khaki-green bamboo stalk as a crutch, I hobbled through the villa and to the front door. As soon as my hand bones twisted the brass doorknob, my ear bones nearly shattered at the sound of Elvira's sharp yell.

"Where are you going?" she demanded.

I turned around to see her beady eyes penetrating my skeleton, steam gushing from her pierced nostrils, and her hands square on her hips.

"I need a doctor. Maybe get some X-rays. The ankle bone isn't healing."

"Fine." Then her demeanor abruptly shifted from demonic to angelic. "I'll be waiting for you, *amore*."

I knew she'd be waiting—with my dog tag, ready to throw it into the netherworld if I didn't return.

Opening the door, I made my way down the beach. "The nearest hospital shouldn't be far," I said, comforting myself, as I hopped on my left foot bone, supported by my bamboo-stalk crutch. I'd heard the hospitals in Costa Rica were among the best in the world. I didn't doubt it, as I'd made my rounds in the country many times and saw the first-rate medical care delivered to patients here. I had a chance at healing the fracture. But this time, I'd enter the hospital as a patient, not to collect souls.

I'd remembered a small, one-story, mustard yellow shack during one of my earlier excursions with Elvira. A blue caduceus, the medical symbol with two snakes coiled around a winged staff, was plastered over its lemony-painted walls. It must have been the local clinic.

The Costa Rican sun shone hot, beating down on my bones. So, I took a route through the jungle, trying to find a shortcut to the clinic. The thick canopies of trees and coconut palms provided the shade I needed to stay cool and comfortable, despite the pain in my ankle bone that worsened after being viciously assaulted by the savage goth vamp, Elvira.

The hiking paths carved into the jungle floor made my trek less arduous and rather convenient. When I glanced up into the treetops, smiling sloths greeted me. In the distance, tourists screamed joyfully as they zip-lined from tree to tree. Flashes of yellow flew overhead, which I immediately identified as being fiery-billed aracari toucans. My ear bones picked up the birds' squeaky calls. The Caribbean wind rustled between the dense vegetation, grazing over my skeleton and cooling my bones amid the humid conditions of Costa Rica's rainy season.

As I hobbled on one leg bone on my makeshift crutch, a small hut with a dry palm leaf roof appeared off the side of the trail. Two scruffy chocolate brown dogs ran out, wagging their tails and jumping on me.

"Down, boy!" I said a few times, until they calmed down. They looked at me and ran toward the hut, then turned back at me again, as if asking me to follow.

I did as the furry canines bid me to do. Not having anything on me but my bamboo stick and cloak, I had no morsels to offer them. It seemed to matter little, as they were friendly anyhow.

Not far from the hut stood a square structure, about three feet in height, hand-built out of bricks, and looking something like a ceremonial altar. Purple flowers sprouted up all over the area surrounding it.

The dogs led me to a bigger hut, circular in shape and also covered by dry palm leaves that acted as a roof. The rain started to pour, and I took cover under it for about an hour.

Once the rain slowed to a mere drizzle, I ventured out again. I hadn't gone too far when the dogs started barking and a short man, his skin as dark as coconut husk and his long hair as silvery as a moonbeam, appeared out of nowhere. He wore a beard and hair neatly combed with a side part.

I didn't expect to see anyone in these parts, far from the touristy areas and in the thick of the jungle.

"Who are you?" I asked.

"Ah, you have come," he replied, his voice gravelly yet gentle. His warm eyes crinkled at the corners of his weatherworn face.

"Uh, I have?"

"Sit." The old man motioned me to take a seat on a flat rock, as if it was intentionally placed there for sitting. Not knowing what to expect, I sat still, watching the man's every move.

He gathered some of the purple flowers and then hovered over flourishing green shrubs and healthy vines twirling tightly around the barks of the trees. He picked the longest, greenest leaves off one by one and dropped them into an earthen bowl.

Too mesmerized to ask what was going on, I sat absorbed in my out-of-the-ordinary experience.

The man lit a small fire, poured water into the bowl, then boiled the concoction for a few minutes.

He walked up to me and offered me the bowl with two hands. "You drink."

My brow bone arched. “What?”

“I, shaman. You, heal.”

How did he know? It must’ve been my bamboo crutch that tipped him off. Indeed, I needed a lot of healing, and this Costa Rican shaman was promising to give it to me.

I instinctually accepted the bowl and looked at the reddish-brown liquid inside. It exuded a strong odor, like that of burnt coffee mixed with damp earth. If it tasted as bad as it smelled, I was about to find out.

In the quiet and calm of the jungle, I brought the bowl up to my mandible and tilted it inward.

Upon drinking the potion, a peace overwhelmed me.

Becoming slightly ecstatic, I asked him, “What is this?”

He smiled and touched my rib cage with his index finger. “Ayahuasca. Good for you.”

I felt an immediate connection not only with this shaman but with the jungle surrounding me.

Lying my cloaked skeleton on the ground, I entered into a deep state of relaxation. Nothing mattered, not my problems, not my pain, not Elvira. A growing feeling of euphoria overpowered my entire skeleton.

Then I saw her.

Through an opening in the jungle that led to the sapphire-blue sea, the beach came into clear view. A small speck, leaping up and down, appeared, then grew larger until I could make out what or who it was. I’d recognize that fiery red hair anywhere. It was Life! She trudged across the shallow bottom of the sea, moving fast toward me. She outstretched her arms, as the curls in her red hair bounced like a hundred summer beach balls. Her voice golden, she called out, “Reaper, I’ve come to save you!”

I stood up, disbelieving that this gorgeous cosmic force was coming to rescue me from the pits of hell. Who was I but a lowly reaper caught in an abyss created by a goth fiend. But unmistakably, salvation was in my midst, as vivid and clear as daylight. I dropped the earthen bowl and sprinted, parting the unruly vegetation in my way. My feet bones dug into the sand as I ran, picking up speed upon nearing the shore toward beautiful Life.

She raced closer and closer, thigh-high in clear seawater. She splashed and called out my name every few feet. The rapturous way she kept saying, “Reaper!” electrified all my two hundred and six bones. I rushed toward her, as fast as my leg bones could take me. It seemed to take forever to reach her. At long last, her body and my skeleton collided in a passionate embrace that took me out of the next world!

Suddenly, I felt myself being lightly pushed. “Senor, wake up,” he kept saying.

The bowl of ayahuasca still rested in my lap. I spun my skull around. “Where is she? Where is she?”

“Who?” the shaman asked.

“The love of my existence. What have you done with her?” I pulled the shaman up by the collar of his plaid short-sleeve light-blue shirt.

"Senor, no one here. You hallucinating."

I set him down. I didn't believe him. I had felt Life in my arm bones, her skin and hair dripping wet like diamonds from the sea. The dampness of her body against mine had moistened my cloak.

"It's dry!" I exclaimed, feeling my cloak for any moisture. "Dry as the desert."

Disheartened, I peered into the shaman's brown eyes, kind and patient, like those of a man who'd lived a thousand years and knew each kernel of truth that ever existed.

Then I collapsed on the flat stone.

Wait a minute. I hadn't used my bamboo crutch, not when I furiously shook the shaman and not when I sat down. Confused, I examined my ankle. The fracture had disappeared.

My jaw dropped.

I stood up. "No pain!" I shouted and leaped in joy. The shaman had completely healed me.

"How can I repay you?" I asked with a grin that went from ear bone to ear bone. "I have no money, no colones. But I want to give you something of equal value to the healing you've given me."

The old man, his darkened face lined with years of life experience, simply said, "You pay it forward. Do good service to someone. Enjoy good existence." He smiled and nodded. "Gratitude from you, good energy. It is fair payment for my services."

I thanked him profusely, not just for healing my bone but for enlivening my dream.

My hallucination of Life may not have been entirely real. But that euphoric vision of ultimate redemption and the shaman's honest soul awakened something in me.

As I turned to go, he gently laid a hand on my arm bone. "The boat give you everything you need."

Huh? A mere boat? What did he mean? I brushed off his cryptic words.

Leaving the shaman, I was determined more than ever to get back to Life by Sweetest Day.

I didn't know how, not yet.

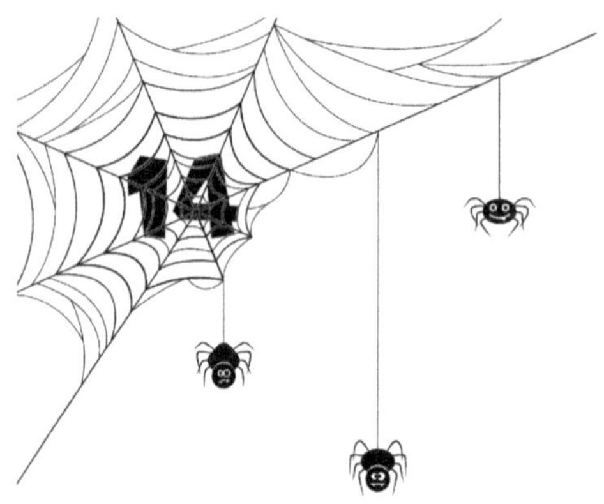

The local repair guy worked on the boat all morning. The parts had finally arrived, and Elvira had scheduled the repair service right away. He replaced the fuel filter and cracked fuel line, then added fuel stabilizer to keep the fuel line free from buildup. His handiwork ensured the boat didn't break down in the middle of the Atlantic, stranding me on board in Elvira's dreadful black claws.

A few hours later, she yelled out, "*Grazie*!" The boat serviceman walked away, smiling and flipping his oil-stained fingers through a thick wad of hard cold cash.

"Reaper, oh Reaper!" Elvira called in her nasally voice as she entered the villa. "The boat is ready. We must return to Italy, where our love will begin!"

I came out of hiding from behind the potted fern, which had grown three feet during the five months I'd been trapped in Costa Rica. "Oh, Italy? But it's so far," I whimpered.

"Pack up the boat," she ordered, glaring at me with her beady black eyes.

Scared stiff, I didn't move a bone.

"Now!" she screamed and stomped her boot, like a raging bull ready to attack the matador strutting in the center of the bullfighting ring. But there were no thousands of eager spectators to watch livid Elvira bunting me with her sharp horns and defeating me in plain sight.

Shaking in my bones, I glanced around, struck by the sheer amount of stuff. Living amid the deluge of goods in the villa for several months had desensitized me to the hoarding. Now that she demanded I move every useless thing onto the boat, my skeleton nearly crumpled into a pathetic heap on the spot.

Every corner in the villa was packed with the frivolous merchandise Elvira had bought on our daily excursions to the various markets. Things she didn't need or ever used in my time here. Piles of clothes, beach towels by the dozens, hundreds of wood carvings large and small, and bags and bags of the prized Costa Rican coffee teetered in stacks from the ceiling to the floor on two levels. Given the stupendous number of plush towels, Elvira apparently had a thing for them. How many did a woman need?

"But there's so much stuff," I whined.

She gave me the Elvira glare. Her coldness sent shivers down my spine.

"All right," I said with a hopeless sigh. With my shoulder bones drooping, I got to work.

I'd start with the heavy lifting first, to avoid tiring myself out right from the beginning. This meant loading up the boat with countless five-pound bags of exotic Costa Rican coffees. Granted, a dolly would've helped tremendously, but I didn't have one lying around.

So, I began the grueling task of packing the boat with only my bare hand bones.

During the transports, I rummaged through everything, making sure Elvira didn't notice. "My dog tag has to be somewhere," I muttered under my breath as I stealthily searched every box and bag I handled.

Time stood still. I hauled coffee bag after coffee bag from the pantry in the kitchen, climbed to the tops of the mountains of them in the living room, and lugged the ones stacked outside on the patio to the boat. I panted heavily as the morning sun shone on my dry bones and I traversed from the villa, across the sandy beach, and to the boat. My heel bones dug deeper into the sand as I carried heavier items, making the trek doubly taxing. The irregular grains of sand under my feet bones demanded I exert more energy than I could muster. After hours of vertebrae-breaking work, sweat saturated my cloak.

By the afternoon, my posture assumed a semipermanent stoop. I didn't get a lunch break and dared not ask for one. I already knew the negative answer I'd receive. Elvira wouldn't have survived a day in the corporate world without a human resources department protecting her. She was clearly on the wrong side of the law—in every way imaginable.

In the evening, three-quarters of the goods were on the boat. While the villa appeared more spacious, the boat became too crowded to move around in. The mountains of stuff made for unbearably cramped conditions. And my dog tag and phone were nowhere to be found.

Coffee bags lay all over the deck, stacked in numerous five-foot-high piles. Fluffy beach towels made opening the door to the cockpit a struggle. Bottles of hot sauce blocked the red-and-green navigation lights. I didn't know how Elvira would steer without clear visibility. Wasn't there some kind of maritime law to protect boating passengers? How safe would this fifteen-day journey to Italy be? The last thing I wanted was to end up caught in the merciless grips of the rough Atlantic, when I was already caught in the pitiless grips of a goth temptress set on sailing me toward a marriage made in the infernal regions.

I could barely move a bone in the cabin. It was crammed with shopping bags, boxes, trinkets, towels, skimpy clothing I dared not imagine Elvira parading around in, and a gargantuan amount of Arabica coffee.

Elvira didn't complain one bit from the deck. She was on a mission, and nothing—not even the threat of the boat capsizing or swamping with all this stuff—could stop her.

By nightfall, the boat was fully overloaded and ready for its voyage. I dropped off the last box and stood inside the cabin, in between tall stacks of boxes, scratching my skull. I could run off with the boat this minute. The keys had to be somewhere here. I'd travel via the Gulf under the cover of darkness and toss all the towels, Arabica coffee, and black skull bikinis overboard, thereby stabilizing the boat and saving fuel. In two weeks, I'd be safely back on the US coast and have at my leisure an entire month to spruce up my bones for the second-biggest night of my life—Sweetest Day with unforgettable Life.

But I couldn't bring myself to do it. Elvira still had my precious dog tag in her possession. She'd expose me without hesitating, bringing an end to my fantastic, long-lived career. I'd be banished, never working for Death again or seeing Life's gorgeous face in the office. I couldn't bear the thought of not being near Life for the rest of eternity. My empty chest cavity crushed, I crumpled onto the cabin floor. My helpless skeleton laid on the cut-pile carpet for nearly a half hour.

Elvira plodded onto the boat. The stomping of her heavy boots unsettled me. "Ugh, she's here," I grumbled, rousing myself.

The engine started.

"Yoo-hoo! Reaper?"

The stamping of Elvira's boots sounded at one end of the boat, then to the other. In seconds, her ankles became visible on the steps leading down to the cabin. She peeked in, her face full of new piercings in places I never dreamed could be pierced. "*Amore mio*! Where are you?" She didn't manage to fit entirely into the cabin, since it was overwhelmed with her hoard of belongings.

"Are you ready, *amore*? We're off to Italy!"

"I-I'm here." My crackling voice came out weak from the back of the cabin, the massive boxes muffling the sound of my reply. I didn't want to sail to Italy, not now, not with her, not on a stable boat, not on any boat.

"All right, *amore mio*!"

I watched as her thigh-high black faux leather boots disappeared up the steps.

The engine revved, and the water splashed against the stern. I crouched next to a large box, with another big box on the left side of my skeleton, and yet other ones behind and in front of me. I was sandwiched for the entire, dismal fifteen-day voyage to Italy.

Even though I hadn't found it yet, my dog tag lay hidden somewhere. Elvira would never leave behind such valuable collateral in the villa, if she wanted to keep me around. It was all I needed to get my hand bones on and be out of here.

But where in the afterworld was it?

We sailed into Portofino and docked in its splendid port.

"You live here?" I asked, as earlier we'd been neighbors farther south of here.

"It's one of my houses," Elvira replied with her pierced nose up in the air and a haughtiness about her. She strode off the boat, as I followed, hunched over carrying a box on my vertebrae.

"Bring the rest of the stuff inside."

One of her houses? What did she do for a living? I didn't dare ask, unless I wanted a bone broken or at the least be nastily yelled at. I dutifully focused on my task.

Just as I'd loaded up the boat in Puerto Viejo, I unloaded it here in Portofino.

Upon bringing in the first box, I gawked at the shiny trinkets everywhere inside Elvira's house. The walls shimmered with incandescent gold colors. A sensuous painting of angels by Peter Paul Rubens hung over the white marble fireplace and another of the severed head of a snake queen draped on the opposite wall. Elvira's artistic tastes had a peculiar duality, kind of like her personality. Lit sconces gave the home a warm yellow glow and plush white-and-black animal skin rugs laid on the floor, as if the unlucky zebras had been on the chase a minute before.

My eye sockets popped at the luxury she lived in!

I couldn't take my gaze off the marble Greek sculptures, their soft bodies twisted unnaturally, the four-tiered black crystal chandeliers hanging from the high ceiling, and the slight darkness that pervaded the home, giving it a sort of eerie, cave-like atmosphere.

With each box, pile of towels, or bags of coffee I brought in, something new and exciting inside the house caught my eye socket. It was like entering a bone-chilling wonderland, full of magic and mystery.

By nightfall, the docks in Portofino lit up, and I'd unloaded the last box into its final resting place. I stood outside the house, taking in the view. The calm water shimmered a midnight blue, as lights from the port reflected off the surface. Dozens of sleepy boats, large and small, docked in the port, as if preparing for a long, restful night. Lush green hills rose up beyond the port, surrounding us. I inhaled the clean, refreshing Mediterranean air. It was cool and crisp. A chilly wind blew, and my bones shivered.

"Time to go inside."

As soon as I entered, Elvira ordered, "You'll sleep in the guest bedroom downstairs. I'll take the upstairs bedroom." She twisted her body coyly and flapped her dark lashes at me. "But only until we're married." She clasped her hands and giggled.

Ah, just as in Puerto Viejo, a clearly orthodox hostage-taker. I brought my hand bones together, looked upward, and gave thanks.

Exhausted after a night of shifting boxes from the boat to the house, I slipped under the blue silk sheets in the king-size bed and fell into a deep slumber.

A large package was delivered the next morning.

"My dress. My wedding dress!" Elvira exclaimed, as I sat in the kitchen, unmoved, drinking a cup of, what else, Arabica coffee.

"I ordered this six months ago. I must try it on!"

Elvira held the black gothic dress up to her chest. Black lacy splotches were sewn into the long sheer black sleeves in random places. It looked a bit chaotic, and suited Elvira to a T. The top half sported a crew neck neckline and the entire thing was chopped off at midsection, with frayed edges to boot. Hmm, a crop top wedding gown. Definitely first-class. My eye sockets zoned in on the cluster of dead red roses decorating the center of the waistline—a foreboding of the doom that awaited me.

"But you mustn't see me in it before the wedding," she squealed, turning to me. "It's bad luck."

What did she know about bad luck?

Elvira ran upstairs with the dress and stayed there for a while.

In the meantime, I dozed off in the living room on the blue baroque couch, its cushions hard as a flat rock. As I napped, I dreamed of a black widow spider crawling up my arm bone. It was massive, black as night and with eight glossy legs stretching longer than its venom-filled abdomen. One bite, and it'd inject its neurotoxic venom into me and send me into delirious spasms. I felt the spider crawl inch by inch up my arm bone. Fearing a deadly attack, I awoke and jumped to shake it off me.

"Tsk-tsk."

I heard Elvira's voice and looked up. She stood above me, holding a tape measure in her fingers with jet-black nails, long as the legs of the deadly black widow spider.

"Stop moving."

"What are you doing?" I asked, bewildered, wondering in what manner she was going to assault me, this time with her tape measure.

"Your arm bones are sixteen inches long."

"And?"

"I'm measuring you. I'm ordering your tuxedo, *amore* mio. Relax." She looked at me, as if her secretly measuring my bones was normal and expected, like buying ice cream on a summer day.

I shook my skull. "Listen, Elvira. I'm not really a tux guy. I prefer a cloak. I've always worn one, seven hundred years and counting now. I can't—"

"Shush!" She glared at me sharply with her beady eyes, each one resembling the venom-filled abdomen of the deadly black widow spider. I could've sworn I saw the red hourglass-shaped spot of the spider glow in the middle of Elvira's eyes. "You will wear a tuxedo on our wedding day!" She stormed off, flipping her long dark hair over her shoulder.

Things didn't necessarily improve after that. Elvira dragged me along on all her shopping trips over the next several days. She apparently needed to buy accessories for our, ahem, wedding.

First, she insisted we shop for her garter. Out of the endless choices, she homed in on one made of crinkled black satin with a silver dagger and crossbones dangling off a little black satin bow.

A dagger, humph. It was no surprise Elvira gravitated toward it, among the gazillion safer options.

She wanted to pull together her gothic wedding look, so she then hovered over a case of headpieces and hair accessories. She picked up a sequined black veil with a generous tail, maybe ten feet long, which I was sure I'd step on and rip, leading to the wedding day being my last.

"*Amore*, what do you think about this veil?" she asked holding it in front of her face.

"Black does really conceal flaws." Coughing, I corrected myself immediately. "Not that you have any, of course," I said with a smile. Wearing a wedding veil, as far as I knew, was intended to ward off evil spirits and anything that drove the bride to dreadful unhappiness. I ventured to wonder about the opposite: what protections did the groom enjoy? I could've certainly used a veil. Perhaps it'd repel Elvira.

She picked out a black crystal-studded tiara with metal spikes jutting dangerously out of it, as if it was ready to stab any witless soul who accidentally got in the way. What gothic wedding was complete without this symbol of the loss of innocence?

"We need confetti, *amore*. Lots of it!" Elvira placed a bulk order with the merchant.

"How could I forget the candles?" She said, looking at tall, elegant slim ones and thick, shorter black ones, secured in glass candlestick holders. Needless to say, she bought the store's entire stock.

She pulled me toward a jewelry shop for pieces that would've solidified our union. "Ooh, look at those glittering black diamonds," she exclaimed, pointing to the glass cases housing gothic wedding rings. She told the salesperson that she wanted the ring with the round black diamond surrounded by ten-karat black gold. She slid it on and admired its glisten under the store lights. Elvira didn't hesitate to pick out my ring too: a solid black gold ring carrying a diamond-eyed skull crowned with genuine diamonds.

I tried to tell her that jewelry wasn't my thing. "Listen, Elvira, the ring's sophisticated and edgy, and I'm flattered by the skull. But my finger bone isn't exactly made for wearing a weddi–"

Her nostrils flaring, she banged the jewelry box on the glass case and cracked it. The salesperson nearly called security, but Elvira showed her a fat wad of cash and averted making a bigger scene.

Browsing for vow books was next. "We must remember our vows to each other, *amore*. It'd be such an embarrassment if you didn't. What do you think of this one?" she asked, picking up a black leather one with a skull engraved on the cover. She clearly had a thing for skeletons.

"It'll keep our vows safe for always," she said, while flipping through another that read Til Death Do Us Part.

I groaned, then opened my jawbone, about to respond.

She immediately turned away, flailing her arms, and raving about a floral wedding arch. "This is perfect!" Then she spotted the dark faux flower decor sitting next to it, dropping the metal arch already in her hands. "Or how about a nice black rose circle arch to show the endlessness of our love?"

I thought I'd offer my opinion but decided against it. She didn't notice.

All the while she was preparing for the biggest day of her life, I was wondering how I was going to get out of the soon-to-be worst day of my existence.

"How are we going to be married without a priest?" Elvira cheerily asked. "Come, let us find the perfect priest to perform our beautiful wedding."

"Eh?"

She pulled me by the hand bones and led me to the nearest church up a hill. The early September morning blew cool breezes as we ascended. We reached the two-story building built in a Romanesque architectural style, and laid with yellow stone upon yellow stone, within a half hour. I glanced up, to be greeted by a small window arch above the doorway. Elvira pulled open the heavy green double doors, with facades of heavenly beings cavorting. The loud, groaning creak of the doors startled me.

We entered. As I waited inside on the black-and-white checkered tile floor, Elvira spoke a few words with the receptionist, who'd welcomed her and agreed to help her obtain the assistance she requested.

A few minutes later, the receptionist waved us into an office. A priest sat in a green leather swivel chair behind a polished wooden desk. I observed the dark mahogany shelves scattered with random books, some with slim spines and others that resembled thick textbooks. Oversize posters of religious rendezvous hung on the rich brown walls. On the right corner of his desk sat a white marble sculpture of an ancient gladiator stabbing a lion growling in agony.

"Who does your decorating?" I asked the priest, trying to make casual chitchat.

He eyed me over his spectacles. "I do," he said sternly, without blinking.

My bones shuddered a little.

Elvira began to voice her request.

The priest listened patiently. He kept glancing at me during his conversation with Elvira. She was rather animated, her arms flying and her eyebrows arching. The priest didn't seem to mind her numerous facial piercings or her onyx fingernails that must've grown two inches and pointier since I last looked.

Clearly taken by Elvira's charm, he pulled her aside. They stood in the corner of the office under a single yellow ray of the sun that streamed through the window. The priest, clad head-to-toe in black, and Elvira, also clad head-to-toe in black, strangely appeared to have an ethereal air. I did a double take, then distracted myself by admiring the plant next to my seat.

In hushed tones, the priest began to express his concerns. He kept looking over at me, as I sat by the potted plant, hearing every word as clear as day.

"Elvira, dear," he said, holding her hands in his. "I am a bit concerned and have some reservations about performing this marriage." He glanced over at me, then returned his attention to Elvira.

"You see, my dear, I suspect that your fiancé is trying to force you into a marriage you do not want." He glanced in my direction, as I pretended not to hear and stroked the green leaves of the plant, admiring their healthiness. He pushed his spectacles up his nose bridge. "Just look at him. So grim."

"I consider myself to be a very, very good judge of character. Now, Elvira, your fiancé appears to me to be the awfully controlling and abusive type. If he ever causes you unhappiness, you come to me. You hear?"

The priest cleared his throat. "No offense, deary, but I cannot perform a marriage when one party is pushed into it against their will."

My ear cavities perked up. Against their will? If only he knew a fraction of the truth!

The priest dropped her hands. "I'm sure you will understand," he said with a soft, grandfatherly smile.

Elvira returned his cordialness with her pleasant black-lipstick smile. Then I followed her, shoulder bones hunched, out the door.

Upon exiting the church, Elvira switched from charmer to ghoul. "Who would ever force someone into a marriage they didn't want?" she bellowed, loud enough for passersby in the square to stare. "Can you imagine someone stooping so low?"

I was about to tell her no, I couldn't imagine anyone doing anything of the sort but refrained.

She pushed onward, her black boots stomping over the cobblestones. "Humph! We will find another priest, a better one." She huffed and puffed and dragged me to the next church.

Our stop took us three blocks away, to a quaint, striped building with a single tower for the church bells. A white clockface appeared at the top of the tower. Above the door was a round, lonely window designed in an innocent floral style. We climbed the two sets of eight maroon steps.

Once inside, Elvira made her inquiry, and we waited.

The priest finally arrived and took us into his office. This time, it was brightly lit with sunlight pouring through the open pink shutters. The walls were painted stark white, and the room appeared rather sparse. The priest sat behind an orangewood desk, and I sat on an upholstered orange armchair. The entire office reeked of pipe smoke, which made me crave for a puff.

Especially in contrast to the prior one, this office appeared a bit plain and boring, with no posters to look at or odd sculptures to ponder. But the ruddy-cheeked, plump, outgoing priest chatted vivaciously with Elvira as I sat quietly, hunched over, trying to pull my hood as far over my skull as possible.

He pulled her aside too. Just like the last time, I heard every word I wasn't meant to hear.

"Elvira, you are extraordinarily lovely and healthy," the priest started. He glanced at me, then resumed speaking with Elvira. "But are you sure this marriage can be consummated? Excuse me for my forwardness, but just look at him. He's all bones." He gazed at me with pity, as I quickly turned to the window to watch a seagull fly across the blue Mediterranean sky.

After a few minutes of discussion, Elvira grabbed me by the arm bone and yanked me out of my chair. She stormed out the church doors and into the street. She didn't say a word about the last encounter. Instead, she muttered, "Do you know how hard it is to find a good priest these days?"

We traversed several more blocks to the other side of town, where another church stood on a hill. Upon climbing up and losing our breath, we reached the top. Elvira walked inside, dragging me along by the sleeve of my cloak.

"Can I help you?" asked the silver-haired receptionist.

"I'd like to ask the priest to perform my upcoming wedding," Elvira answered with a smile.

"Certainly. Follow me."

She took us through double glass doors into an office. The burly priest leaned his chin on his palm, examining the papers scattered across his desk with intensity. Behind him, on the wall, was painted a triangle with an eye in the center. The luminous colors surrounding it radiated in all directions.

What was someone like Elvira doing in a blessed place like this? I reminded myself, I unfortunately knew.

We took our seats and again, Elvira posed the same question.

Sighing, the bald priest, with a few straggling white hairs, appeared worn and tired, as if he'd been scrutinizing papers all afternoon.

This time, I didn't wait for them to hold a private discussion. I got up and walked over to a gold-tone baroque frame on the opposite side of the room and pretended to enjoy viewing a painting of the marriage of heaven and hell. Despite me standing several feet away, Elvira's and the priest's words sounded clear as rock crystal.

"Now look, Elvira. You strike me as being highly responsible. I am sure you will make a fine wife someday." Then he looked up at me from his desk. "But him," he said, twisting his lips and speaking in a whisper, "I'm not so sure he's capable of handling the duties of marriage."

The priest patted the top of Elvira's palm, as if she'd been a good girl. "I want you to be happy and well-cared for,

Elvira. But your intended groom doesn't seem to me to be someone who can stand up to the challenges of marriage." He shook his head. "I'm sorry, Elvira, but I must decline."

Elvira gave him a small smile and we left.

I sighed in relief at my good fortune. That was three priests in one day who'd refused to perform this marriage. Wasn't it a sign to Elvira that this wedding wasn't supposed to happen?

One last church lay within walking distance. It was at the far end of town, an immense, whitewashed church with multiple tall steeples reaching high into the late-afternoon sky.

We climbed the endless sets of gray stone steps, entered the church, and were shown into the priest's office. Dead tired, I collapsed into the chair.

The slender young priest stood up and extended his hand to vigorously shake Elvira's. She made her request, and he immediately grabbed the phone off his desk to check his calendar app.

"I'd be happy to perform your wedding. But marriage ceremonies are common, you know with young people excited to enjoy matrimonial bliss for life." He looked at me and winked.

Eh? Matrimonial bliss? What realm did he come from?

"I'm booked on Sweetest Day," he said. "Seems it's a popular day to get married. How about the fifth of October? I'm free. It's the only day I'm available anytime soon."

Elvira's charcoal-lined eyes popped. "Yes! We'll take it!"

The agonizing cry from the recesses of my skeleton came out as a light gasp.

And so, it was settled. The dreaded marriage was moved up to the fifth of October, two weeks away.

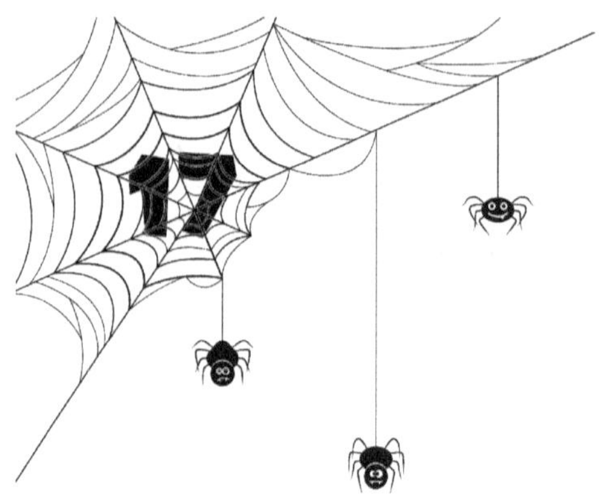

The wedding venue was next on Elvira's list.

"*Amore*, since the marriage has been moved up, I'm having second thoughts."

My brow bone arched. "Oh?" My empty chest cavity palpitated. My bones slightly tingled. Maybe this wedding would be called off. Elvira had finally come to her senses.

But she yapped on. "Instead of a church, we shall be married on the pier, right here in beautiful Portofino!" She threw her arms up in the air in a jubilant show.

Turning to me with glistening, yet still beady, eyes, she exclaimed, "My boat, made doubly handsome with your name across it, will be in the backdrop." With sweeping moves of her hands in front of her, she imagined out loud, "I see it now. Our wedding ceremony on the pier with my boat in the backdrop. *Amore Reaper*! It's the perfect photo op!"

Goodness gracious. All I needed was a professional portrait photo of us, her arms wrapped around my resisting skeleton, suffocating the air out of me, and capturing a love that never existed and never will.

As the wedding date fast approached, Elvira rushed to make the preparations. The flower arch arrived on her doorstep. She had chosen a metal arch bent in the shape of a horseshoe—which didn't, up to this point, ward off my ill luck. Large blooms of black and dark purple roses poked out of every open crevice in the arch, creating a perfect picture of awaiting doom.

The day before the wedding, Elvira hurried out, with the wedding arch in hand, toward the pier. She placed the tall black candles, supported in glass candle holders, on the wooden planks of the pier, creating a sort of lengthy border in the place where our dreaded union was to take place.

She'd bought a hundred bouquets of black roses and lined them in an equally large number of black skull vases along the pier. The sea of black flowers competed with the shimmery blue Mediterranean Sea itself. The bouquets emerged from openings cut neatly into the tops of the skulls, making me feel a little uncomfortable and wonder about my personal fate should this marriage take place.

It was bound to happen, because I hadn't yet found my dog tag—the one piece of collateral that hand-bone cuffed me to this abominable situation. If I located it, I could escape without fear of my crush on Life being found out and jeopardizing my career. Plus, my dog tag held sentimental value. It contained the photo of our first outing together. It wasn't any old office photo with the whole team grinning silly for the camera. Engraved into my dog tag was an intimate picture of stunning Life and me, alone, during the most incredible night of my existence. It was irreplaceable, and I had to get my hand bones on it.

During the entire evening before the dreadful ceremony, all Elvira chatted about was how glorious her boat would look in our wedding photo. "*Amore Reaper,* just as my boat says." In her excitement, she tried to pinch my cheekbone, but, consisting of 100 percent bone, she naturally failed.

"No one has ever had a wedding on the breathtaking Portofino pier with a boat, named after her soon-to-be husband, in the background. We are special, no, *amore*? The most amorous couple ever!"

I turned to respond, wanting to comment on how especially horrible it was, but she yakked on about her boat and the photo op. I hoped no one would ever see said photo, but knowing Elvira, she'd enlarge it to poster size, frame it in a golden baroque frame, and hang one copy in every room in her gigantic house.

“And then we shall have our first kiss, on the pier, in front of the boat! We shall make it a long one, *amore*, and win the Guinness World Record for the longest kiss ever!”

I covered my eye socket with my hand bone. This couldn’t truly be happening.

“A bride must get her beauty sleep. I will rest. You wouldn’t want to see me tomorrow standing before you at the altar with puffy bags under my eyes. Wish me good night, *amore*, and we shall be married tomorrow!” She threw her arms wide and pranced up the stairs, as if she were waltzing to the sounds of my miserable silence.

I sat dumbstruck in the living room, unable to move a bone. I was trapped without an escape route in sight. If I didn’t find my dog tag tonight, I’d be a very unhappy Mr. Elvira tomorrow.

All Elvira had yapped about was her boat. The boat with my name on the hull. The boat for the wedding photo op. The boat this, the boat that. All nonsense that signified nothing.

As her obsession with the boat strangled my hopes, leaving me gasping for freedom, the old Costa Rican shaman strangely appeared in my mind’s eye socket. I couldn’t help but to fixate on his words to me: “The boat give you everything you need.”

The boat will give me everything I need? How would it give me my freedom, a freedom that would soon be torn from me, leaving me in the merciless grips of ultimate destruction and unending gloom?

His words stuck in my mind, circling around, as I dropped into bed, twisting and turning until midnight.

Then, my skeleton shot up in bed. "The boat! That's where my dog tag and phone must be hidden. It has to be! I've looked everywhere else but there."

I threw the blue silk covers off and tiptoed to the bedroom door. I pressed my ear bone against it. All was quiet, except for the raucous sounds of Elvira's wall-shaking snoring from upstairs.

I returned to the bed and tucked three pillows under the sheets to mimic my sleeping skeleton, just in case Elvira wandered down.

In the still of midnight, I snuck out of the house and toward the pier.

The boat floated in the dark blue water of the port. Subtle yellow glows shone from the buildings surrounding it. A few boats were lit, but Elvira's boat remained dark. I hopped onto the deck in my black cloak, camouflaging me against the nightscape.

"Where could it be?"

I scratched my skull. I'd spent mortifying amounts of time down in the cabin for weeks, twice, and there was no sign of my dog tag or phone anywhere.

I crept toward the stern and entered the cockpit. Numerous controls, screens, and levers—all new to my eye sockets—surrounded me. I'd never been inside a modern boat's cockpit. The only boat I had access to was the plain ancient one in which I'd long ferried souls. It didn't offer the magnificence of empowering controls, a leather-trimmed steering wheel, or a cushiony, leather-backed swivel chair. I was impressed, even a little envious. Why didn't my boat feature a multitude of controls to ease the final journey, a luxurious steering wheel for my age-old hand bones to grip, and a cup holder? Giving my clients safe passage to the next world would've been a treat for me and made their ride an enjoyable, even unforgettable, experience. I made a mental note to myself to bring it up with Death later.

I returned to my critical task. Upon searching every inch of the cockpit, thrusting my arm bones into the deep shelves and drawers, my hand bones came up with nothing.

Then a small gray metal box peeking out from under a red-and-black cloth at a bottom corner caught my attention. It laid near where Elvira's feet would've been when she steered the boat. There was no way I'd have gained access to it when she was around.

Curious, I uncovered it and peered closer. A small hole, like for a key, came into view under the warm yellow lights of the port.

"I don't have the key. Drats!"

I searched around the cockpit, looking into every nook and cranny. Maybe the key was somewhere here. But Elvira wouldn't have left the key to the safe lying around.

"Hmm."

A reaper hack was in store. I took my pinkie bone, inserted it into the keyhole, and gave it a wiggle. I heard a click and the safe unlocked.

I opened its door. Voilà! "My precious dog tag!" It was here all along. I grabbed it and kissed it and looked up to the sky with an outpouring of relief. I scooped up my phone lying next to it.

Tucking both items into the inside pockets of my cloak and buttoning it closed, I shut the safe.

I thought to run off at that instant, with my dog tag and phone, at last, in my possession. I had what I needed to make a clean, quick escape and never have to face Elvira again.

But emotions overwhelmed me, and I hesitated.

Strange feelings—feelings for Elvira—overwhelmed my skeleton. With my dog tag and phone tucked safely into my inner cloak pocket, I sat on the maroon steps outside her home, deep in contemplation. It was October 5. The dawn over the event she'd been anticipating for an excruciatingly long time had finally risen. "Should I go?" I asked myself. It'd been what I wanted all along for the past six months of this torturous hostage situation.

But I'd grown to know the sum of Elvira, the good and the bad: her quirks, her silliness, her abusive nature. After all, in a fit of rage, she'd willfully doubled the size of my ankle bone fracture. I still recalled the unbearable pain: throbbing, intense, and one I wouldn't wish on anyone else.

She had a softer side though. She wasn't always horrifically abusive and maniacally controlling. Maybe once we got married, she'd somehow transform into someone who was perpetually charming. Love made so many things possible. Was this love or some morbid obsession? It was hard to distinguish at this moment of do-or-die a second time. Elvira's black-lipstick smile and facial piercings, in places I'd never dreamed imaginable, gave her a sort of uncommon quaintness. Definitely, Elvira was one of a kind.

Wouldn't someone like me be proud to call her my wife?

Plus, she was loaded. She lived in a mansion, owned another home farther south, and claimed even more houses across the country. She could afford a boat and a pay for a two-story villa on the spot. I could exist in the lap of luxury if I married her. I suppose I could've easily overlooked her demanding nature, her physical and verbal abuses, maybe even disregarded her selfishness—if I got to reside in a palatial space like this, on the shores of gorgeous Portofino, under the clear blue Mediterranean sky.

As I weighed the pros and cons, Elvira's shrill yell pierced the still morning air. It was almost ten o'clock, when the ceremony was scheduled to take place. "Reaper! Why aren't you in your tux?"

I needed more time to think. I screamed out, "It didn't fit. I'll see you at the altar!" and ran to hide in the small wooden shed in the backyard. Mansion or not, I wasn't about to change out of my frayed cloak and into a fitted modern tuxedo paired with a crisp white tuxedo shirt, and a black silk bow asphyxiating my neck bones. Formalwear, nope, not for me, not for the next world.

From the crevices between the faded wooden boards of the shed, I spied Elvira. She pranced through the doors of her house in her lacy black crop top wedding dress. Her muffin top spilled out. Flattering, indeed. But she looked gothic as ever: head-to-toe in midnight black, from her wispy wedding veil at the back of her head down to the vamp of her military boots.

I emerged from my hiding place. I straightened my cloak, smoothing out the random wrinkles. Standing tall, I made my decision and headed for the pier.

The priest waited at the altar. He gave me a taciturn nod and quickly looked away.

The Mediterranean breeze blew over the port of Portofino. It was a temperate seventy-five degrees. The sun drifted upward diagonally, without a dark cloud in sight. Seagulls screeched as they flew across the sky. Fishermen crowded on the pier, casting their nets and lines for fish and lobster.

Elvira's boat floated a few feet away. The lettering, *Amore Reaper*, appeared crisp and clean, as if it'd been painted yesterday. It'd be a nice photo op, certainly. The wedding photographer might even take a second portrait of Elvira and me posed on the bow pulpit. I quivered in my bones.

The priest smiled at Elvira as she approached, marching steadily down the pier to the calming sounds of the

Mediterranean water, in between the black roses stuffed in black skull vases, with dancing flames from the black candles lighting every step of her unhurried procession.

She carried her black flower bouquet, moody and mysterious, like her.

As she marched, her face winced. The fishermen had begun cheering. They'd just reeled in a majestic, flapping king mackerel. The men, dressed in canary yellow waterproof aprons, navy blue knit hats, and gray sweaters, hooted and hollered as they next hauled in their wire traps, filled with half a dozen snapping lobsters.

Elvira twisted her lips at them, then looked forward in our direction, putting on her sunny smile and pretending not to notice the loud commotion disrupting her wedding.

The priest and I stood at the altar, stupefied as to what to do.

Then came sounds of loud splashing. The fishermen yelled and danced a jig, having pulled in an impressive load of speckled sea trout and amberjacks from their gillnetting. The fish flapped their tails, and soon the surrounding air became permeated with the seaweed-like stink of fish.

Elvira and the priest held their noses, while I covered my nasal cavity with my hand bone.

She attempted to shush the boisterous fishermen, patting her arms down and bringing her index finger up to her lips.

As expected, they ignored her and danced and hooted even louder.

At last, she arrived at the altar, the glistening sea before us and the priest ready to perform.

Elvira covered her face with her wedding veil, which heightened her air of mystery. But through the sheer black veil, she smiled her sunny black-lipstick smile. Her beady black eyes twinkled under the morning sunbeams. Every strand of her dark, wavy hair remained firmly in place, giving evidence to the several cans of hairspray she'd used.

As the seagulls squawked and the fishermen cavorted, the priest looked at Elvira and began.

"Do you, Elvira, take this, ahem, *man*," he said, clearing his throat and giving me an awkward, slightly angry, look, "to be your husband, to live together in matrimony, to love him, to honor him, to comfort him, and to keep him in sickness and in health, forsaking all others, forever?"

Beaming, Elvira said, "I do."

Then the priest turned from her to me.

Doubts at once raced through my mind. Was I making the right decision?

"Do you, um, Reaper," he began, coughing, "take this woman to be your wife, to live together in matrimony, to love her, to honor her, to comfort her, and to keep her in sickness and in health, forsaking all others, forever?"

What?

Forever?

His last word struck me in the skull like a forty-pound medicine ball.

I'd never gone through a wedding ceremony before, but I knew what "forever" meant. I'd been there, in the afterworld. Forever was a long time, beyond life, beyond death, into the everlasting infinity of space and sheer existence. Did I want to "keep" Elvira forever? Being mercilessly controlled and unapologetically mistreated. . . *forever*?

The reality sunk in. My rib bones caved in. I dropped my skull to my empty chest cavity. My breathing labored. No one asked me how I was.

At that moment, I couldn't. So, I bolted.

The priest looked up, watching me with a dropped jaw, as I sped down the pier, jumped cannonball-style into the water, and dog-paddled to the boat.

"Wait, *amore mio*! But our marriage!" Elvira screamed, chasing after me, reaching out with one hand, and clutching her black flower bouquet in the other.

Soggy, I climbed aboard her boat and scrambled to the cockpit. Using my pinkie bone, which came in handy during dire emergencies like this, I started the engine. In seconds, I sped off across the water.

I looked back. Elvira came charging after me. She was knee-deep in the sea, her black wedding dress soaked and the flowers from her bouquet scattered in the water. She'd thrown back her veil, likely to get a clearer view of me as she tried to reel me back in to certain, everlasting doom.

Adding more horsepower to accelerate the boat, I made progress. I looked back one more time, only to see Elvira go under the water, with one arm reaching up and the bottom of her gown floating on the surface, like a terrifying black sea monster, as she cried out, “Reaper, amore mio!” Then, nothing.

I returned my focus to the dashboard as the speeding boat’s dials spun out of control. I had a mission: take Life out on Sweetest Day. And I had exactly fourteen days to reach the States.

Despite being inexperienced in manipulating the sophisticated controls of the boat, I managed to navigate it out into the crystal clear Ligurian Sea. Off to the north rose majestic views of rugged cliffs and picturesque seaside cities.

The waves bounced as I pushed onward. The air grew chilly, and the nighttime temps fell to the fifties. I gathered my cloak around my neck bones for warmth. Besides my hand bones, they were most exposed to the bleak sea weather.

A few hundred miles later, I sailed past Nice and the French Cannes.

It didn't take long until I sped past Barcelona and crossed the Balearic Sea.

Upon reaching the Alboran Sea, the narrow Strait of Gibraltar came into view. Rolling green hills clustered on my left and right. The strait stood as an eight-mile-wide watery, blue passageway through which I'd sail the boat before bursting into the unstoppable freedom of the wild Atlantic.

I wasn't worried about this British overseas territory controlling the passage of my boat, as I wasn't smuggling or illegally transporting goods. On the other hand, Britian should've been more attentive when Elvira resorted to unlawfully kidnapping me and transporting me through its narrow waterway.

Let bygones be bygones. I had new problems now.

Boats and cargo ships crowded the strait. I had to be extra cautious sailing past the three hundred or so ships that passed through daily. Every five minutes, my eye sockets caught at least one vessel making its way through. The last thing I wanted was to crash my speeding boat in one of the busiest waterways on Earth. Being a newbie piloting a contemporary boat, I wasn't too sure I'd make it.

I sailed the Gibraltar Strait with my knee bones knocking. My brow bones lifted at sightings of rare marine life. Friendly bottlenose and striped dolphins swam alongside my boat, as if they were my marine angels, ensuring I passed through safely. I pressed my hand bone on my rib cage and sighed.

As I approached the point where the Mediterranean Sea and the Atlantic met—the Europa Point—its famous tourist attractions beckoned me. The Europa Point Lighthouse, from where I could spot Morocco on a clear day like this, stood tall and proud. I wished to explore the Ibrahim-al-Ibrahim Mosque, an architecturally brilliant gift from the king of Saudi Arabia. Who gave mosques as gifts? If Elvira had the heart, she might've used her bottomless well of cash to build and gift one.

But my date with Life held more importance. I cruised along steadily.

It took three days to sail across the dense waters of the Mediterranean. During my time in the saline sea, I experimented with the advanced controls and levers. I'd never piloted a boat featuring an intricate, high-tech control unit before. Considering my lack of experience, I did a fine job.

I immediately got used to the throttle and shift functions. Driving the boat using the single-lever controls delivered incredible freedom, as I discovered I could work the engine with one hand bone and turn the steering wheel with the other. The boat's digitized controls gave me a definite advantage. Plus, ever since my recent conversion to all things tech, I found the electronic control system delightful.

My boat, which I use to ferry souls across, failed to offer even the semblance of exciting mechanical controls. I did all the work myself, as I'd done for the past seven hundred years. Passage consisted of manually rowing the boat with a wooden oar, and my client sitting at the other end, patiently tolerating the lack of technology that would've streamlined their transport to the next world.

My face bones turned red as I recalled all the souls I'd previously ferried across in my outdated boat.

As the boat sailed into the Atlantic, I brought out my phone—thank goodness it came with waterproof features—and jotted into my notes app all the shiny bells and whistles I wanted for my next boat.

Death hadn't given me a boat upgrade since I started my career. I was long overdue for one.

First off, my current boat needed an electronics system to enhance safety and navigation. I could even entertain clients on my boat with it. A nice side-scan sonar would provide a detailed view of the water as I ferried souls across. Heck, even I never knew what lurked beneath those murky waters.

My existing boat lacked a console, but a blackout dash would be an elegant addition.

While I was at it, I typed in that a sound system with lighted, neon-colored speaker rings and a subwoofer would be appropriate for creating an enjoyable atmosphere my clients would remember long after they stepped off my boat to the other side.

"There," I said, finishing up my notes and tucking my phone back into my pocket. I'd text Death my notes as soon as I got the chance. My priority was getting back to the States in time for my date with the incredible, unforgettable Life.

So far, I'd managed to learn how to manipulate the various controls and gears. Though intimidating at first, operating the boat was now a breeze.

Or so I thought.

The Atlantic grew rough. The weather shifted rapidly, producing strong winds. The boat no longer traveled at the speed it had sailed through the Mediterranean. Controlling the boat became difficult.

I didn't know how fast I should go. So, I slowed down the boat. It seemed like a good idea, until the boat became stuck in the troughs. I sped up, trying to reverse my mistake. But it was too easy to lose control.

Traveling the choppy Atlantic took more mental and physical stamina than I imagined.

Sleeping more than fifteen minutes at regular intervals wasn't an option. A cargo ship could've approached in the middle of the night and run over the inconspicuous boat and me. Tropical storms brewed heavily in October, threatening to capsize my boat and leave me stranded in the Atlantic with little chance of rescue. Who'd transport me to the next world? Me? I gave it no more thought.

Loneliness consumed me. A mental breakdown was imminent under the overcast skies and all alone in the vast ocean. I also didn't know this boat very well. Though, I gradually grew accustomed to her.

Crossing the blue ocean in a tiny boat would be an event I'd never forget—given I managed to avoid a second death.

If I made it to the US coast, it'd be out of pure, dumb luck.

Sleepless and tired, I stood at the helm, night and day, steering the boat, trying to avoid freight ships and tropical storms and staying on top, rather than under, the rough waves.

The challenging conditions of this transatlantic voyage weren't my cup of tea. But I remained determined to be with Life. Otherwise, she'd be lonely and wondering—and I didn't want anything of the sort.

It'd been fourteen days, meaning it was Sweetest Day. I wasn't sure I'd make it to Life's door on time. But I'd given Death my word. I checked the time on my phone: three o'clock. I pushed the throttle forward, accelerating the boat to its maximum speed.

All went well, until it didn't.

A sea stack appeared out of the sudden big waves, jutting a hundred feet out of the choppy water, which had hidden it from view. I couldn't look and brought my hand bones over my eye sockets. But I had to pay attention to survive. Trying to avoid hitting the rock head-on, I swerved the boat abruptly.

My swift maneuver was too late. The boat flipped, crashed into the rock tower, and shattered instantly into pieces.

Hurled off the boat, I fell into the water.

My skeleton floated to the surface, with my cloak acting with existence-saving buoyancy. As water splashed into my mandible and I gasped for air, I was forced to make a quick decision.

A long, wooden piece from the boat wreckage drifted by. I grabbed the broken part and used it as a floatation device. I wasn't a good swimmer and needed all the help I could get.

The only good thing about this terrible situation was that I wasn't far from shore. Flutter-kicking my leg bones rapidly, I hung on to the wood and inched toward shore.

It took hours of kicking.

At last, I reached the beach and scrambled into the neighborhood, reaching Life's door at precisely 6:59 p.m. for my seven o'clock date. Panting, I rang the doorbell.

Life answered, smiling and beautiful.

"Reaper! You're soaking wet!"

"What are you up for?" I asked, after explaining I'd spent some time at the beach.

"I feel like singing!" Life replied, her emerald green eyes sparkling. As always, she looked stunning, in her chic ruched mustard yellow dress that hugged her every curve.

"Karaoke it is!"

Upon wringing out my cloak, we headed toward the local karaoke club.

It was packed with people hungry for a chance to belt out their favorite tunes on stage for a bunch of random strangers. I eyed the abstract futuristic paintings hanging on the walls. The floor was a kaleidoscope of geometric shapes. Moving strobe lights lit it up. Under the dramatic show of neon purple and blue beams, I sat on the perforated leather seats with gorgeous Life at my side.

Folks sprang up onstage, holding the mic in their hands and singing today's hottest music as the lyrics rolled on the wide screen.

How did these amateur singers know every word to the songs? It was as if they'd listened to them on repeat or something.

Life gave me a slight nudge with her elbow. "How about it? You first?" she said with a wink.

How hard could it be to jam onstage—and impress Life with my lyrical gymnastics?

"There's nothin' to it." I hopped up onstage and took the mic. I forgot that I wasn't a fan of today's music, not pop, not country, not the blues. I simply didn't have the time.

Nevertheless, I picked an old eighties tune, and the music started.

From below the stage, Life moved to the rhythm, bopping her knee. Her brilliant, gemlike eyes looked up at me. Her jaw opened slightly, as if to gasp.

I was a rock star.

As the music played, I realized I was about to perform in front of a huge crowd of onlookers, anticipating my song as much as Life did.

A paralyzing feeling overcame me. My skeleton grew tense and fidgety. I became lightheaded. My empty chest cavity pounded fast. I'd never sung karaoke in front of strangers or anyone.

The first few lyrics crossed the screen.

My eye sockets widened. I began to feel nauseous. The crowd cheered me on.

All I could do was hum to the tune.

The people screamed, "Come on!"

I needed to perform. I took a spot on the stage that someone else might've wanted. So, I forced myself to sing, but my voice came out shaky. Only my mandible fell open a little to utter a couple lyrics. My eye sockets veered to the left, then to the right, scanning the jeering crowd, as my skeleton froze.

They started to boo.

The room began to blur. A tightness grew in my throat bones.

Without warning, Life leaped onstage, grabbed a mic, and belted out the lyrics to the song. Her voice came out strong, melodious, and powerful. She looked at me with her sultry eyes as she sang, and the music swelled in my chest cavity.

I joined in, loud and somehow in tune.

Together, staring into each other's eyes and eye sockets, we sang in unison, "With you, I'm having the time, the best time of my existence!" Our duet turned the club upside down. People hollered and threw their arms up in the air, reaching out their fingers to touch Life's dress and my cloak.

Three minutes later, we finished the song, our arms and arm bones wrapped around each other and the crowd screaming, "More! More!"

"What'd you say?" Life asked with a smile.

"Why not?"

Under the hot stage lights, Life and I sang our hearts out again. Tune after tune, the crowd lapped up our performances. Sweat glistened on Life's skin, and my bones shimmered with beads of sweat.

At last, laughing and holding on to each other, we skipped off the stage.

"That was a blast!" Life said.

"I never knew you could sing!"

"Oh, it was nothing. Something I do in my off time."

We headed over to a quieter spot and sat down at the table for drinks. The server brought us a bottle of champagne, two beers, and a couple glasses, and then took our orders. Life popped the cork and poured champagne into her glass. I drank my beer straight from the can.

"Whoo-hoo! Death is missing out on a lot of fun!"

"There's no question Death's not getting any rest, with the epic monsoon he's setting up in Bangladesh," I said, my nasal cavity inhaling the aroma of the bowl of grilled veggie nachos coming our way.

"Oh, he's always off doing something grand. It's just like him." Life crunched on the cheesy nachos that had just been served along with other starters. We munched on the mozzarella sticks and pickle chips.

Life's Cobb salad with blue cheese crumbles and guacamole arrived, and she dug her fork in.

I satisfied my palate with a jalapeño house dog, complete with onion ketchup and relish.

It didn't take long for us to clean our plates after working up our appetites onstage.

"I need to go to the bathroom," Life said, after our meal, and excused herself from the table.

This was my chance to text Death. I brought out my phone and began to text.

> Reaper: Boss, could you text me the latest schedule? I know you're in the middle of a monsoon, but I'm done reminiscing about the good ol' days. Thx.

I tucked my phone back into my pocket, just as Life returned.

"The music's slow. How 'bout we dance this one?" she asked.

Taking her arm, I led her to the floor. We slow-danced in the dim atmosphere, her warm body against my now mostly dry cloak.

As she rested her chin on my shoulder, I took out my phone to check it from behind her. Still no text from Death. I needed the latest schedule, which listed the most recently departed clients I had to pick up. I anticipated one particular soul—whose place on the list secured my freedom.

Life and I slow-danced to a few more songs.

I kept checking my phone as we danced.

Life stopped, pushed her body back, and cried out, "Reaper, you keep checking your phone!"

"Oh, I'm sorry. I'll put it away. Just work, you know."

She gave me a warm smile, and we continued dancing the rest of the night.

As the club was about to close and we were on our last dance, my phone chirped.

Death had texted me and attached my latest schedule.

Death: OMG. The monsoon is EPIC!

Whoopee, more souls for me to collect.

I reviewed the schedule not once, not twice, but three times.

Exasperated, I cried out silently.

"Elvira. . .is not on my list."

My jaw dropped.

Thank you for reading *A Morbid Obsession: A Grim Reaper Comedy Adventure*.

If the grim reaper's lively antics tickled your funny bone, share your thoughts in a review!

www.riyapresents.com

www.ingramcontent.com/pod-product-compliance
Lightning Source LLC
Chambersburg PA
CBHW071942190726
48293CB00004B/1309

9781956496475